MESCALI⟶⟵⟶

ROCKY MOUNTAIN SAINT BOOK 13

B.N. RUNDELL

WOLFPACK
PUBLISHING
— EST 2013 —

Mescalero Madness
(Rocky Mountain Saint Book 13)

Paperback Edition
© Copyright 2019 B.N. Rundell

Wolfpack Publishing
6032 Wheat Penny Avenue
Las Vegas, NV 89122

Paperback ISBN 978-1-64119-821-9
eBook ISBN 978-1-64119-820-2

To my readers, one and all. Thank you for sharing your time and joining me for these short rides into the past to gather memories to take into our future together. Thank you.

CHAPTER ONE
WATER

"I've eaten enough dust these last three days so I prob'ly won't be hungry for a week!" declared Tate, spitting and wiping at his eyes and neck. "And if I find me a bath in Santa Fe, it'll end up muddier'n the Mississippi!" Tate Saint was talking to John Bernard, the man that was the leader of the long line of freighters bound for Santa Fe and the owner of the trading post that awaited the promised goods. Tate had scouted for him before, but that was to take wagons to Fort Laramie in the territories.

A dusty face with mud daubs at the corners of his eyes looked back at Tate, grinned with weathered and cracked, dry lips, "All the more reason for you to find us some water yonder!" as he pointed to the landmark known as Point of Rocks. "It's a little off the trail, but if there's water, we'll shore do it!" he declared.

With a nod and a wave, Tate nudged his horse away from the wagons now traveling four abreast toward the distant knoll. It had been an unusually dry and warm winter in the Sangre de Cristo Mountains west of the Cimarron Cutoff of the Santa Fe trail, and the flats now traveled by the many freighter wagons had yet to show the characteristic green of spring. Tate Saint started for the Point of Rocks just south and west of the Round Mound. Their crossing of the sun-burned flats had been unexpectedly dry, and their last crossing of a riverbed had yielded only another layer of dust for the famished travelers and their animals. That had been the Rabbit Ear Creek, and their stop at the usual camp found only a trampled mud bog where the spring usually offered fresh water. Now he was hoping the spring at Point of Rocks would be sufficient to slake the thirst of their struggling teams, but he also knew the wide mesa was often been used by the Comanche as a hunting camp.

His long-time companion, Lobo, the wolf he found as a pup and had been with him since, led the way, his easy loping trot leaving puffs of dust with every step. Tate was astride his blue roan grulla, Shady, and was scouting for the freighter wagon train coming from St. Louis and bound for Santa Fe. This had been an unusual trip with more than the typical challenges. With the Civil War in full swing, they were often challenged by groups of both uniformed and guerrilla fighters, but since the way had been through Union territory, those challenges were nothing more than temporary inconveniences. But in the last several days, they had rebuffed highwaymen pretending to be Union Guerrilla fighters and had a running confrontation with a war party of Kiowa; now they were passing through Comanche country. But Tate had been a friend to the Comanche in years past and hoped this would be enough to see them through to the mountains.

But now his thoughts were on water. If there wasn't enough at the Point of Rocks, it would be at least another day, perhaps two, before they would reach the Canadian River. The bone dry, brittle, brown grass moved in the morning breeze as Shady pushed his way through the knee-high buffalo grass and each step kicked up more dust. As he neared the landmark of the outcropping of rocks, the long wide mesa lay like a shadow behind but nothing showed promise of water. Although this was his first time on this part of the trail, he had quizzed the old-timers that had traveled this way, and like many men of his time, the landmarks were imprinted on his mind as if there were a map laid out on a table before him. The pointed knoll reminded him of a Spanish sombrero with the point of rocks in the middle, and the wide brim turned up around. The spring was supposed to be to the left or south of the knoll with a small pond surrounded by gnarly cottonwoods. Usually, he would see the green of the trees and other vegetation, but everywhere showed pale brown.

He pointed Shady to the shoulder of the rocky ridge that promised access to the top of the knoll and leaned forward as the horse dug his hooves into the dry soil. The steed hunched his back and pushed hard with his heels to make the last few yards of the steep climb and grabbed at the crest with his hooves to make it to the top. Tate had been focused on the climb, and when they crested the ridge, he was surprised to see the camp of several Comanche around the small pool of water. Four mounted warriors blocked his way, two with arrows nocked and bows slightly bent. One man, hand uplifted and palm forward, came forward to confront the apprehensive Tate.

Before the man spoke, Tate greeted him with, "A-ho!" holding his hand up and palm forward as well. He continued in the language of the Comanche people, "Are you from the village where White Feather is the Shaman and Raven is the chief?"

The surprise on the face of the man was evident, but he responded, "Those who you speak of have crossed over, our Shaman is Buffalo Running, and our chief is Ten Bears. Who are you to speak of our people?"

"I am Longbow." Tate used the name he was given by the Kiowa chief, Dohäsan, because of the English Longbow he used. "I have been a friend of the Yamparika for many years." Tate was known by this name by most of the tribes of the mountains and great plains and had been a friend to many.

"I have heard of Longbow. I am Black Elk. My father, who is known as White Horse, has spoken of you."

"I remember White Horse. We have been in battle together. Tell your father, Longbow speaks highly of him and remembers our time together."

"Why are you here?" asked Black Elk.

"I am scouting for the wagons you see in the flat. We are traveling to Santa Fe, and the rivers have little water. I came to see if there was water enough here for our horses."

Black Elk moved to the side and pointed to the small pool of spring-fed water, "There is not enough water for our people. If you were to bring your many horses here, there would be no water left."

Tate looked at the little pond, seeing the water level was well below the marks on the nearby rocks. "I agree. I will take the freighters on to the Canadian River." He looked to Black Elk, thinking of the other dry riverbeds they had already crossed and asked, "Does the Canadian flow with plenty of water?"

"Yes, and our village made our summer camp above the crossing."

"Then, I will go. May the Great Spirit give you and your people a good summer," said Tate as he reined his mount around and with a hand signal sent Lobo back down the slope to return to the wagons. Although the back of his neck crawled and he wasn't comfortable turning his back on the warriors, he knew he could show no fear and deliberately held Shady back as they descended the slope away from the rocky outcropping called Point of Rocks. It wasn't until he drew near the waiting wagons that he finally breathed easy and grinned as he approached John Bernard.

"So, tell me you found water!" said Bernard, hopefully, waiting for an affirmative reply.

"Yeah, I found water," answered Tate.

"Good! Good!" declared Bernard, but before he could continue, Tate interrupted.

"But I also found a bunch of Comanche that don't want to share their water!"

"Comanche! That's all we need! A big bunch?" he asked, calculating.

"Big enough! 'Sides, ain't enough water for this bunch. I don't think there's enough for even all the men, much less these animals," he answered, motioning to the many teams. "We'll just have to push on to the Canadian."

Bernard snatched off his hat and beat the dusty felt against the pommel of his saddle, leaving his sweat-sogged hair and forehead to catch the breeze and give a brief cooling. He ran the sleeve of his shirt across his brow, leaving a muddy streak on his forehead, giving the appearance of a clown in brown makeup. Tate chuckled, "Ain't gonna do no good fussin' about it, but if we put a bucket on your pommel there, you might catch 'nuff sweat to water your own horse!"

Bernard snarled at Tate, "Ain't funny!" He lifted his eyes to the bright sun that shone as if it was the middle of July instead of the beginning of April. "That sun's sappin' the strength of all the animals and the men too! It's more'n a day to the Canadian and we ain't even sure it's got water!"

"It does, them Comanche have their summer encampment upstream of the crossing, and they said there's water."

"You talked to 'em?" asked the trader, dumbfounded.

"Yup. And from up there, I could see the bed of the Ute Creek. Now, I don't think there's any water there, but there might be some greener graze for the animals, and that'd help. We could stop there and wait till after dark to continue. That way it'd be a little cooler and easier on the mules! What say?"

Bernard looked to Tate, thinking, then answered, "I reckon that'd be best. Go 'head on an' find us a camp. We'll take a meal, get some rest, and head out after dark. There is a big moon, ain't there?"

"Ummhumm, not quite full yet, but big 'nuff," answered Tate. From the time of his first journey to the west, Tate had preferred to travel at night, believing it to be easier on his horses and he enjoyed the quiet and solitude of the darkness. As a student at his father's knee, he had learned about the stars and the directions and could just as easily find his way at night as in the daytime. As he gigged his mount to take the lead of the wagons, he let Shady have his head, and he settled back to rock to the comfortable gait of his trusted mount.

Seeing the Comanche brought back a flood of memories of when he first came to the mountains. As a youth, he and his father had dreamed of going to the Rocky Mountains, but after his mother died and his father was killed by a crooked card sharp, he had to live that dream by himself. He and his father had been students of the history of warfare and were fascinated with the English longbow, so much so that they crafted one each and mastered the use of them. It was to be a skill that would serve him well and earn him the name among the native peoples. But now, after many years, he had become known as the Rocky Mountain Saint, taken a bride and was now a parent to two children, both mostly grown. Now he was responding to a call from an old friend and mentor, Kit Carson, to be a scout for the man who had joined the Union and was already a colonel in command of the First Regiment of the New Mexico Infantry and serving under General Canby.

Tate wasn't much for this Civil War business and all the conflicts that seemed to create even more conflict, but he was loyal to his friends, and Carson was the first he made in the Rocky Mountains. Now he was needed, and he was on his way to do what he could for his friend. But only time would tell about how much he would become involved in the fighting, and he wasn't too inclined to be shooting at other white men that might just disagree with his thinking.

CHAPTER TWO
DESERTERS

THE FIRST STAR TO LIGHT ITS LANTERN WAS IN THE EAST, AND IT twinkled to life in the grey blue of early night. The big moon that waxed to full took his place to show his rugged complexion with the familiar blue glow. Other stars soon followed suit as Tate mounted up for the night's scout. Lobo and Shady were anxious for the trail and the familiarity of night travel bode well with the two while Lobo, tongue lolling and a smile that split his face, trotted back and forth, excitement showing. Tate swung aboard and slipped his Spencer into the scabbard. He turned to look at John Bernard, "As long as the trail's easy to follow and there ain't no trouble, you won't see me. If the trail gets dim, I'll stack some rocks to point the way. As you know, some o' them arroyos can be tricky, but I'll scout 'em out good."

"Wal, if'n we make good time, we should get purty close to the Canadian, mebbe even push on a little after first light, if we hafta," responded the wagonmaster.

"With this dry dirt makin' powdery dust, I reckon you'll be traveling three or four abreast?"

"Yeah, long's the cacti don't get too thick. Them patches of beehive, prickly pear, and hedgehog can do some damage to a mule, so if'n you see a big patch, stack some rocks or sumpin' so we can miss 'em."

"Gotcha! Will do."

With a nod and a wave, Tate reined around, and pointed Shady to the trail with Lobo already on the run into the night. Tate chuckled to himself as he watched the wolf disappear, knowing full well that part of his enthusiasm was the hope of finding a girlfriend for a little midnight rendezvous. It wouldn't be the first time Lobo went courting, but he also knew he would hear the lonesome howl of romance that would also be Lobo's way of saying 'don't wait up.'

Tate let Shady have his head, and he looked into the night, checking shadows and letting his eyes develop the necessary night vision. With the moon near full and a cloudless sky, not only could he see, but he could also be seen, so he dared not take any unnecessary chances as he pushed through the darkness. It was about an hour later when he heard the first long lonesome howl that came from a slight knoll before him. He recognized the clarion call of Lobo and reined up to listen. There was no answer, then Lobo let out another, also unanswered. Tate put an easy heel to Shady's ribs, and they moved out.

With an occasional stop to mark the best place to cross an arroyo or to show a hazardous patch of cacti, he made good time. It was always pleasant to hear the barking yip of the coyotes, also looking for romance, the rattle of the cicadas and the occasional burrowing owl asking his question of the night. But Shady moved silently in the soft soil, and it was only the creak of the saddle leather that told of any movement until something caught Tate's eye and he pulled the horse to a stop. In the distance, maybe just over half a mile, the winking light of a small campfire showed itself at the edge of a small flat top mesa. *That's gotta be a white man, ain't no natives gonna have a fire in the open in the middle of the night. 'Sides, it ain't even cold!* Tate shook his head as he thought of some pilgrim that was more concerned about pushing back the darkness or maybe having coffee in the middle of the night and wasn't even thinking about sending a signal to any raiding Comanche or Apache.

He sat for a while, searching the moonlit flats for any indication of others, man or animal or any other danger that might be imminent. In these times and this country, trouble seemed to raise its ugly head just when you least expect it, but since he was the expecting kind, it wasn't going to take him by surprise. He listened for the sounds of the night, heard the peent-peent of the nighthawk and in the distance, another pair of coyotes sang to each other. He was satisfied the creatures of the darkness were not alarmed, and he gigged Shady forward.

He chose to approach the fire from the edge of the mesa, keeping the bluff behind him. He tied off Shady to a scrub piñon, and with rifle held easy in the crook of his arm, he moved quietly toward the ring of light. There was a picket line of six horses, saddles stacked nearby, each marked with CSA. From behind a stunted juniper, Tate surveyed the camp. The men were arrayed like spokes in a wheel with their feet to the small fire that now licked at the last of the wood, hot coals glowing in the small circle of fire. With five in their blankets, one man sat dozing, staring at the fire as he leaned against a big rock that had fallen from the rimrock of the mesa and now made a good backrest for a nodding lookout. The guard was in the grey and butternut of the Confederate army, but was unkempt in his appearance, giving Tate the belief that these were deserters. He knew there had been a couple of battles, but those were on the west side of the mountains, and the last he heard, the boys in grey had left the country, headed for Texas.

Tate looked at the fire, saw only a coffeepot and three cups, no frying pan or pot that would tell of other food. There were no packs near the saddles and no haversacks by the sleeping men, so these men were low on supplies and probably lost as well. He stepped forward and called out, "Hello, the camp!" The man on guard jerked awake and jumped to his feet, bringing the rifle up as Tate called again, "Whoa there, I'm friendly! Alright if I come in and get a cup o' that coffee I smell?" He looked at the others, and only two were stirring, the rest still snored soundly.

"Come 'head on, only keep your hands where I can see 'em!" ordered the guard.

Tate walked slowly forward, rifle cradled in one arm and the other hand lifted. "Just passin' through an' smelled the smoke and then the coffee. Had ta' stop an' see if'n I could beg a cup."

"What'cha doin' travelin' at night?" asked the guard, relaxing a bit as he watched Tate seat himself on a rock near the fire.

"Safer that way. Most Indians ain't movin' around, less'n they're up to no good. But it's nice an' quiet. With that full moon," he nodded toward the light overhead, "I can see most ever'thing I need to or want to. S'alright?" he asked, reaching for the coffee pot.

The guard nodded but didn't lower his rifle. One of the sleepers that stirred sat up and looking at Tate, asked, "Who're you?"

Tate looked at the man, grinning, "I'm Tate Saint, an' you?" he asked.

"I'm Smitty, and that's Jonesy!" nodding to the guard, "What're you doin' in our camp?"

"Gettin' me some coffee."

"That ain't what I meant. I mean what're you doin' here?" he demanded.

"Well, friend, something you might want to consider. Folks out west here think anybody that asks a lot of questions is plumb rude! Folks out here kinda mind their own business. But, since you asked, I'm scoutin' for some folks comin' along the trail back yonder."

Smitty stood and looked into the darkness, thinking he could see what Tate was talking about. Tate shook his head, grinning, and sipped at the thick java. When the man turned back to look at Tate, "I don't see no wagons! 'Sides, they wouldn't be travelin' in the dark!"

Tate rested his elbows on his knees, his rifle across his legs and the cup near his mouth, he casually slipped his Colt from the holster and held it out of sight. He looked at Smitty, "That's somethin' else that folks are mighty careful about out here, an' that's callin' a man a liar. A fella could get killed for that." Tate looked at his now empty cup and leaned forward to set it down. "Now, the way I got it figgered, you fellas are deserters from the Confederacy, and you've been wanderin' around with no idea where you are or what kind of danger you're in."

"So what if we are?"

"It doesn't make any difference to me, cuz I ain't one for uniforms and war an' such, but you're in the middle of Indian country, and you're between two different camps of Comanche. Now, that campfire there is like waving a red flag at a bull and just darin' them fellas to come lift your hair."

"What'chu mean, lift our hair?" asked Jonesy.

Tate noticed the other men stirring, one got up and went to the trees and was returning. "Where 'bouts are you fellas from, the city? Ain't'chu ever heard 'bout Indians scalpin' folks?"

Smitty reached up to run his fingers through his hair and looked to Tate with wide eyes.

Tate looked from one to another of the men then asked, "Do you fellas know where you are or where you're goin'?" When they looked at each other, Tate had his answer, then continued, "And from the looks of things, you don't have much in the way of supplies either, am I right?"

Smitty nodded as he hung his head, "Yeah. We been camped here for two days, an' ain't seen nothin' we could take for meat. An' we don't know where we are, either. We were with the Fourth Texas Mounted Rifles under Major Raguet at Glorieta Pass. We had outflanked the boys in blue, an' then we were on what we called Sharpshooter's ridge and was pickin' 'em off purty good, but then we got pushed back, and another bunch attacked us from the rear, so me'n these boys decided to head for the high lonesome and took to the trees. For a while there, we thought we had beat 'em, but they kept comin' and the last we seen, our boys was hightailin' it for Santa Fe."

Tate grinned, "Well, they prob'ly had quite a welcome there, 'cause a friend o' mine was at Fort Marcy with four regiments of troops. So, I reckon your outfit's probably hot-footin' it back to Texas."

Jonesy looked to Smitty and asked, "So, what're we gonna do?"

Smitty hung his head, shaking it side to side, "I dunno," he answered, quietly.

"Do you wanna go back to Texas?" asked Tate.

"Wal, that's home, so, yeah," answered Smitty.

"Tell ya' what, fellas. I've got a little bit o' pemmican and cornbread in my pack an' a little bit o' coffee. I'll let you boys have that, but you need to take outta here right away, 'fore them Comanche come sneakin' up on ya'. If you head that'away," he pointed to the southeast, "and travel after dark, you should be in Texas in, oh, three, four days or so." He stood and started to the trees to bring Shady to the circle. He emptied his haversack before the men, letting them gather up the goodies, tied the empty bag behind his saddle and looked around the circle. "Now fellas, I ain't spoofin' 'bout them Comanche. They catch up with you, you won't be seein' Texas."

"Thanks, Tate, an' we will, we'll get movin' right away."

Tate swung up on Shady, looked down at the men, and with a wave and a nod, he reined around and disappeared into the darkness. He shook his head, thinking about the young men, none probably older than his own son, Sean, and he doubted if they would have enough sense to follow his advice and make it back home. He reached down and patted Shady on the side of his neck, and spoke to his horse, "It's a darn shame, too. This crazy war's got boys leavin' home for adventure, and all their findin' is the end of the road. All because some crazy politicians can't agree on nothin', at least nothin' that's right!"

CHAPTER THREE
CANADIAN

A GLANCE OVER HIS LEFT SHOULDER SHOWED THE FADING EASTERN star, twinkling its goodbye as the horizon showed a glimmer of light that backlit the flatlands, making a long flat line black silhouette. With the grey of morning, Tate sat sideways in his saddle, right foot deep in the stirrup with his left leg crooked over the seat. He leaned forward toward his left knee, looking at the slow coloring of the eastern sky by the lazy rising sun. Pale pinks chased away the deep blue-black to announce the arrival of another day, that promised to be just as hot and dry as the day before. But Tate looked into the wide scar of the river bottom that carried the first running water he had seen in four days. Shady pranced a little to tell of his thirst and eagerness to get to the water post haste. Tate sat back in his saddle, slipped his other foot in its stirrup and with gentle knee pressure gave Shady the go-ahead to go to the river.

At an eager trot, they quickly came to the chuckling waters, and Shady stepped in until all four hot hooves were cooling off in the refreshing river. He stuck his nose in, blew a few bubbles, and lifted his head to swing his forehead mane full of water, back at his rider. But Tate knew his tricks and slipped off the saddle and standing in knee deep water, stripped his buckskin tunic and bent over to wash his torso in the cool, clear water. Lobo had been the first in, and he splashed around, swam upstream and back to his friends, then went to the rocky shore and shook himself free of the heavy liquid.

Tate grabbed his tunic from the saddle, rinsed it out, then walked to the shore to hang it on a nearby alder. Lobo lay in the only shade offered from a stunted cottonwood, and Tate joined him, both watching Shady pawing at the water, turn to look at them, and then blow a few more bubbles. When the grulla joined his friends, Tate stripped the saddle and bridle, dropped them in the shade, and rejoined Lobo to watch Shady cropping at the nearby nubs of grass. He looked over at Lobo, "Boy, you keep your eyes open and make sure Shady don't go too far. I'm gonna snooze a little, so you mind things, y'hear?"

The big wolf cocked his head to the side as he looked at the man, then with ears down and tongue hanging, he smiled and lay his head on his paws, watching the grulla graze. Within moments, Tate's muffled snores came from under his floppy felt hat as his tunic, hanging on the nearby branches, added to the shade.

A low growl brought Tate fully awake, but he did not move. Speaking softly, "I see 'em, boy." He was peering from under the brim of his hat, arms still folded across his chest. He looked side to side, then slowly rose to slip on his buckskin tunic. His Bowie was in a sheath between his shoulder blades and was obscured by the shirt. He strapped on his belt that held his .44 caliber Colt Army revolver in a holster, and his metal-bladed tomahawk at his hip. His Spencer leaned against the large rock that sheltered his other gear. He stood casually, leaning against the boulder and waited as he watched the Union Cavalry patrol cross the river.

What Tate guessed to be a shave tail lieutenant led the group as the horses waded through the deepest part of the river that failed to reach the bellies of the horses. He saw the officer keeping his eyes on him and he waited for the usual greeting, probably some kind of insolent question or order. These green officers somehow managed to quickly develop the attitude that they were in charge of everything, military or not, and that those that didn't obviously out-rank them should snap to and/or jump whenever the officer spoke. But Tate resolved to keep his own attitude in check as he watched the horses rise from the water. The officer quickly stepped down, giving his horse the freedom to shake the water free, but the man turned to Tate, "Who are you, and what are you doing here?" he demanded.

"Well, hello to you too, Lieutenant." He lifted his eyes to the morning sun and continued, "Yes, it does look like it's going to be a nice day. Thank you for asking." He lowered his gaze to the man, a blonde with a "Jeff Davis" hat pinned up on the left side with a feather protruding out the back.

The lieutenant's light-complexioned face and neck showed red at the belligerence of the man before him. "I asked you a question!" he demanded.

"Ummhumm, that's what I thought it was. And, sonny boy, I suggest you start showing a little respect to your elders. I have a son 'bout your age, and if he spoke to me like that, I'd have to take him over my knee and give him a proper spanking! And, well, he's even bigger'n you." Tate stood over six feet with broad shoulders and narrow hips, a weathered-leather complexion and was usually clean shaven, although a few days growth shaded his face now. He bore the scars of Indian fights, grizzly and mountain lion encounters, and a few from cantankerous mountain men. Yet he seldom raised his voice or changed his stance, but he did smile as he looked at the young man and he also noticed a burly older sergeant behind the officer with a drooping red moustache that was fighting to keep from busting out laughing. The lieutenant stepped forward, and Tate thought he could see steam coming from the man's nose and ears, but he waited without moving.

"Are you going to answer my question, or do I have to put you in chains?" The lieutenant was definitely angered but also a little short-sighted. Lobo, now seeing him as a threat, came to his attack-stance beside Tate, growling with head lowered and the hair at his shoulders standing, eyes blazing and teeth showing himself ready to defend his friend.

The young officer jumped back, grabbed for his saber, but Tate stepped forward, hand out as a signal to Lobo.

"Don't do that, he'll kill you sure!" his words sounded like a command and the months of drill and training stopped the man instantly.

The shavetail looked at Tate, down at the wolf, and back at Tate, "That's a wolf!" he announced as he realized the beast before him was indeed a wild animal and very capable of killing.

Tate looked at the lieutenant, feigning surprise, looked down at Lobo, then dropping to his knees and putting his arm around his neck, he spoke into the wolf's ear, "Now, don't you listen to him, boy. You're my friend, and don't you forget it!" He rubbed the scruff of the now relaxed Lobo, stood, and looked at the lieutenant. "Now, maybe we could start over." He extended his hand, "I'm Tate Saint, and you're . . .?"

The young officer looked at him, relaxing his grip on the saber and letting it fall back into its scabbard, then reached out for Tate's hand, "I'm Lieutenant Fairfax, commanding the patrol from Fort Union and the Third U.S. Cavalry, Major Thomas Duncan, Commanding."

Even the first sergeant standing behind the lieutenant relaxed and stepped to the side of the officer, "And I'm First Sergeant Halloran, and it's pleased I am to make your acquaintance!"

Tate shook hands with both the lieutenant and the first sergeant, then explained, "I'm scouting for a train of freighters bound for Santa Fe. Then I'll be joining up with Colonel Carson and his New Mexico Volunteers, wherever they are now, last I heard they were at Fort Craig."

"We're on routine patrol looking for hostiles," explained the lieutenant.

fusils. Only good for hunting." For such a big man, his voice was somewhat whiney and insincere.

"How much?" asked Tate.

"Oh, señor, I see you have one of the new Spencer rifles. I would give you both of these for your rifle!"

"Yeah, I bet you would, but I need my rifle."

"The rifles I traded would sell for twenty dollars each, but I would trade for sixty dollars, gold."

Tate made a dramatic reach as he dug into his pocket and brought out two twenty-dollar gold pieces, looked at them, and looked up at the Comanchero. "Looks like all I got is forty dollars!" He shrugged his shoulders and turned away but was quickly stopped by the big man.

"Señor! Never let it be said that Jose Piedad Tafoya, the Prince of the Comancheros, would pass up a trade. Forty dollars and the hawk in your belt."

Tate lifted his arm to look at his tomahawk as if considering the trade, then looked at the man, "Nope. I need muh hawk. But I tell ya' what I'll do, you give me them youngsters, and I won't tell Colonel Carson you've been tradin' rifles to the Comanche. And I won't tell Ten Bears you've been cheating him and his people on those trade goods."

"You know Ten Bears?" asked the man, concern registering on his face.

"And most of the people in his village, Buffalo Running is also a friend."

The Comanchero held out his hand, looking around to see if he was watched, then said, "Forty dollars. But if anyone asks, you paid eighty!"

Tate grinned and handed to two coins to the man and walked to the two youngsters and cut their bonds. "C'mon kids, you're comin' with me. We need to get you some new clothes and get you cleaned up. What's your names?"

The older of the two, a boy of about twelve, spoke, "I'm Ezra, and she's muh sister, Maribel."

They were tired, hungry, and dirty. What clothes they had were ragged, and their bare feet showed blisters and cuts from the long walk. Both rubbed their chafed wrists and timidly walked behind Tate, furtively looking around for some other attack. "Mister, what's your name?"

"I'm Tate. Tate Saint. Now, tell me, are you the only ones that survived the wagon train?"

"Yessir. We were pickin' berries by the stream when the Indians hit the wagons. I made Maribel hide under the willows with me 'til they left. Weren't nobody left alive an' when I went to check, two of 'em had waited around and saw me and got both of us. That were two weeks ago, and we ain't done nuthin' but walk since."

"Did you get much to eat?" asked Tate.

"No, sir, not much. Just some funny kinda cornbread, and we shared a rabbit leg one time."

"Let's get you cleaned up and into some good clothes, then we'll feed you all you can hold, how's that?" asked Tate, stepping through the door of the general store.

"That'd be mighty fine, sir," answered the boy, shepherding his sister beside him.

After a bath at Mama Martinez' boarding house, and being outfitted with two new sets of clothes, Tate led the two, each carrying a bundle with the spare set of clothes, into the café. When they were seated at the table, Tate looked at the matronly woman that stood with her hands on hips, smiling at the youngsters and said, "Ma'am, these two haven't had a good meal in a couple weeks, so bring whatever you think they'd like and plenty of it, please."

"What kind of a man are you that would starve young'uns for two weeks?" she asked, staring at the buckskin-clad man seated before her.

"Uh, I didn't do it. They were taken in a raid on a wagon train, and we just got 'em back!" declared Tate, defensively, hands held up beside his shoulders, eyes wide as if she was about to attack him.

"Oh. Well, that's different." She looked at the two, "How 'bout some fresh beef stew and some hot biscuits?" Both youngsters smiled and nodded their heads enthusiastically as the woman turned to go to the kitchen.

They topped off their meal with a slice of berry pie each and were happy and talkative as they walked from the café. But they were no sooner on the boardwalk when Tate's attention was grabbed by two drunken men, obviously vaqueros by their attire, that were talking animatedly as they looked toward Tate's grulla that was tethered at the hitchrail before them. Lobo had been told to stay beside the mount and had bellied down in the shade of the horse, but the vaqueros were alarmed at the presence of a wolf. Tate heard the words *matar* and *lobo* and quickly approached the two drunkards. One man had pulled a pistol from his sash and was bringing it up, pointing towards Lobo when Tate reacted. The big Bowie whispered through the air and pinned the man's arm to the support post for the overhead balcony. The knife pierced the man's arm, causing him to drop the pistol and scream. He looked to Tate, anger flaring in his eyes and he shouted in Spanish, waving his free arm and hollering to his companion. The second man was grabbing at his sash for his pistol when Tate, with two long strides, stood before him with the barrel of his Colt under the man's chin. Lobo had come to his feet and now stood, head lowered and teeth showing as he growled at the attackers.

"That's my friend, Lobo, and you're almighty lucky I don't let him tear your throats out!"

"But señor, we did not know," whined the man with the barrel at his chin.

The first man was struggling to free his arm when Tate reached over and jerked the Bowie out, then held the two at bay with both the pistol and the knife. "Now, maybe next time you two won't be drinking your tequila so early in the day?"

"Si, si," answered the second man as he helped his friend down the street for some aid.

Tate called Lobo to his side, went to one knee, and rubbed the scruff of his neck and said, "C'mon boy, I've got somebody I want you to meet." He stood and walked back to the two youngsters, who stood frozen in place as they witnessed the confrontation.

Then seeing the big wolf, Maribel stepped behind her brother, and Ezra said, "It's alright, sis, he's a pet."

BY THE TIME the wagons rolled in, Tate had outfitted the two with a horse and saddle that would carry the pair and bedrolls for each. When John Bernard asked, Tate simply said, "Oh, I picked 'em up for a bargain price. Couldn't resist. Figgered, maybe I'd sell 'em for a profit when we get to Santa Fe."

"I know you don't expect me to believe that," answered Bernard. "But for right now, that's as good a story as any, I reckon."

IT WAS the afternoon of the second day out of Las Vegas when the freighters were on the trail to Glorieta Pass. The roadway had been well traveled by other trade caravans and troops but also led through hostile country. The shoulder that held the road was above the many arroyos that carried rainwater to the Pecos, but below the table-top mesa that shadowed the entire trail to the top of the pass. Dark timber covered the slopes of the mesa but retreated from the roadway, offering little cover in the event of an attack.

Uncomfortable at being exposed in the open below the high bluffs, Tate pointed Shady to a talus slope that led to the top of the mesa, anticipating a better promontory to survey the country. Shady easily mounted the multi-colored clay hillside and topped out in a cluster of juniper well protected from sight. Tate dropped to the ground, slipped his brass telescope from the saddle-bags and ground tied Shady, but with a wave of his hand sent Lobo before him to find a lookout. Tate grinned when he saw the wolf, head high, front feet on a large boulder, and looking at the valley below as if that was his kingdom. Tate bellied down on the rock and began scanning the entire countryside for any danger.

It wasn't until he trailed the edge of the mesa that he spotted movement in the trees at the edge of the rimrock.. He scrutinized the area and spotted several horses tethered in the trees back from the bluff. He watched, waiting, and the slightest movement revealed several figures, also searching the valley, but without the aid of a scope. He recognized them as Apache, but with the different bands and little difference in their dress, he couldn't tell if they were Lipan, Chiricahua, or Mescalero, or some other more obscure band. But there was no mistaking they were Apache with their headbands, trade goods shirts, and high-topped moccasins. Plus, the usual Apache was shorter and stockier than other plains Indians.

He watched, trying to get a number, and finally after counting the horses, he had a good idea this was a small raiding party of no more than about a dozen warriors. He turned to search for the wagons, and the dust cloud to the southeast showed their approach. He didn't think there would be any danger of attack, with twenty wagons, a mule-skinner and a couple of teamsters to each wagon, another five or six with the remuda, all well-armed, that would be about seventy-five fighting men. Quite a formidable force for a dozen Apache. But, as Tate knew, you can never tell about Apaches.

CHAPTER FIVE
APACHE

TATE RODE OUT IN FRONT OF THE WAGONS BESIDE JOHN BERNARD, stopping occasionally to scan the mesa ridge with his scope. "I don't understand it, John. They're shadowing us and letting themselves be seen like they're taunting us or something. Usually, you don't see Apache until they're in your face and screaming their war cry ready to cut your throat!"

"With only a dozen, I don't know what they can do. We've got the train doubled up, and all the men have their rifles ready. It would be suicide for that many to try to attack us."

"Unless they're waitin' for more to join 'em. Mebbe they're just keepin' watch on us until they get more warriors," mulled Tate, sitting sideways using the saddle horn to rest his elbow and hold the scope steady. "Near as I can tell, only a couple of 'em has rifles, and I don't see more'n five or six at a time. Mebbe the others went to get some more to help 'em."

"Don't know, but we best keep movin'. I wanna make the crest of the pass 'fore dark." He shaded his eyes as he looked to the cloudless sky, pointed, "Lookee there!" There was a gathering of turkey buzzards circling, some diving, but that was a sight only seen when there were several dead bodies, animal or man.

Tate looked, "Don't suppose they're still pickin' at the bones from the fight 'tween the Union and the Rebels, do ya?"

"Dunno, could be. I'da thought the bones woulda done been picked clean. From what that trader said in Las Vegas it took 'em a few days to haul in the dead, an' they didn't touch all the animals. He said there were nigh unto fifty dead on each side an' more'n that wounded. No tellin' how many carcasses of horses an' mules there are, but I'm bettin' there's gonna be a stink for a mighty long time."

The rattle of gunfire from the rear of the wagons startled them both. "The remuda!" shouted Bernard. Tate reined around and both men started at a run toward the sound of fighting. The screams of war cries, the whinny of frightened horses, and the cry of wounded men echoed across the valley floor. A plume of dust rose as the horses and mules were stampeded away from the wagons. The herd numbered somewhere between forty and fifty animals; spare teams for the freighters and riding stock for some of the men, but a tempting prize for the raiding Apache.

Three men lay sprawled in the dust, four others watching the dust cloud that told of the escaping herd. Tate and John stopped to check on the men, and in an instant, Tate knew the three down were dead, and two of the others were wounded. He went from man to man to check their wounds, turned to Bernard, "Give me a couple men with Spencers or Sharps!"

John nodded and mounted up to get the men requested.

The boss of the remuda, Johnson, the only handle he went by, shouted, "Them thievin' Indians took Kendall, that young feller with the red top-knot!" He was shaking his fist toward the disappearing herd. He looked up at Tate, "Ya gonna go after 'em!"

"That's the idea!" answered Tate.

"Lemme get muh horse!" he growled and started for the saddle-horses tethered at the rear of the cook wagon.

Tate walked up to the man known as Cooky and asked, "Will you keep an eye on the young'uns?"

"Yessuh, will do!" declared the big, colored man. He had traveled with Bernard on several trade expeditions and was as dependable a man as you could find. He smiled broadly at Tate, "They's ain't no trouble. They's even been heppin' me with the rations an' wanna hep with the cookin' too!"

"Good, keep 'em busy, and teach 'em everything you know," grinned Tate, turning back to the men that rode up with Bernard. Three men, each with the butt of a Sharps rifle protruding from the scabbard beneath their saddle fender, looking eager if not apprehensive, to pursue the Apache and the herd. Tate looked at them, then to Johnson, "Can you fellas hit anything with those?" With nods and grunts, Tate had his answer and reined around, looked down to Lobo, "Let's go!" He kicked Shady into an easy lope and followed the wide dug-up trail of the herd.

By the sign, it was evident the raiders had stopped long enough to give the animals a drink at the crossing of the Pecos, then drove them south along the winding river toward the foothills of table-top mesas. As they traveled, Tate thought, *the rest of the Apache were south of the trail and moving west and are now going south into the table-tops. Either they have a rancheria in these hills, or they're setting us up for an ambush.*

Beside the trail was a sight that brought them to a sudden stop. A big juniper had the lower branches stripped off, and the captive man known as Kendall was spread-eagled against it. He had been mutilated almost beyond recognition. Stripped of clothing, scalped with blood running over his face, his eyes were cut out and ears cut off. Strips of flesh had been sliced from his torso, and a wide slit across his belly let his entrails spill out. The intestines were stretched out and hung below his knees, and Tate knew he had been alive when that happened, but now his head hung in death's surrender.

"Them murderin' savages! We oughta do that same thing to ever' one of 'em," growled Johnson, gritting his teeth. One of the other men was leaning to the side, depositing his breakfast on the ground beside him.

Tate looked at each one, "Remember this, and when I tell you to do something, don't ask questions, just do it."

They were less than two miles from the Pecos crossing, and the herd was following the river downstream through the twisting and winding river bottom that had more green than the animals had seen in weeks. Often stopping to grab a mouthful, the animals had slowed to enjoy the greenery. Lobo came trotting back to Tate, with occasional glances over his shoulder, and Tate knew he had found the raiders. He reined up, looking around for cover and turned to the men, "I'm goin' to take off thataway," pointing to the west of the river toward a series of knob hills, "and try to get a sight on 'em. You fellas move back into that grove of juniper and let your horses get some graze and water. I won't be long, and maybe I'll come up with a plan that won't get us all killed." He didn't wait for a response but gigged Shady to the arroyo that led from the river and would hopefully take him to a good promontory so he could plan their next move.

He pointed Shady to the rocky point of the lower mesa and the grulla dug deep to climb the steep slope. When they topped out, Tate ground tied the horse and together with Lobo, he hunkered down to work his way to the edge of the rimrock. As he neared, he bellied down and they crawled to the edge, scope in hand. Below him, a finger ridge from the mesa pointed out into the river bottom causing the stream to wind around the point and make a horseshoe bend around another point from the other side. Further downstream, about four or five miles, Tate saw twisting wisps of smoke that he suspected marked the rancheria of the Apache. As he moved the scope upstream from the finger ridge, he spotted the herd grazing in a wide grassy flat near the river. They were watched by three mounted Apache, with three or four more near the stream. As Tate glassed the area, he searched for at least one more that would have taken a look-out to watch for any pursuers. They were waiting to set an ambush for anyone following. There, near that cluster of piñon and juniper, lying on his belly and watching from the crest of a slight knoll. One man with another just below the crest, sitting with the leads of their horses in his hands.

As Tate watched, he surmised they would have time to recover the horses if they acted fast and smart. He crabbed back from the ridge, mounted up and keeping to the arroyo bottoms, he returned to the men to lay out his plan. "Now fellas, most of this is gonna hafta be long distance. Can any of you hit anything at about, oh, four hundred yards?"

Johnson looked at Tate, "I done some buffler huntin' an' I can do better'n that!"

Another of the men, a mean looking sort with a lantern jaw and stubbly black whiskers, said, "Can't guarantee nuthin' but I usually hit muh target at that range, sometimes farther." The other two shook their heads and dropped their gaze.

Tate said, "Alright, here's what we'll do . . . now, I'll start the dance, but I don't want you showin' yourselves. Johnson, you take this man," and he looked at the younger of the two, and asked, "What's your name?"

"Taggert," answered the thin rail of a man with brown hair protruding from under his hat and a moustache drooping over his mouth.

Tate looked to Johnson again, "Take Taggert here and move along that side of the river, stay to the arroyos and when the river turns back toward you, sneak a peek and pick your target." He looked to the other man, "Your name?"

"Roberts," he growled.

"And you?" asked Tate, looking to the last man, the youngest of the four with dirty blonde hair and peach fuzz on his chin.

"McGovern, sir."

"Alright, you two," then nodding to the blonde, "an' you follow him," nodding to Roberts, "You two do the same on this side of the river. But keep your heads down cuz the two scouts are on a low ridge keeping a lookout. Wait till I give the signal, then take your shots."

He looked at the men, mounted up and started back toward the ridge. Within moments, he and Lobo were atop the lower knoll that stood above the ridge where the lookouts were. He was behind a stunted piñon as he strung his longbow. When he stepped beside the tree, he knew he would be exposed to the three warriors by the river, but he hoped they would be looking elsewhere. Everything depended on his taking out the lookouts with causing alarm. He nocked an arrow, stuck another in the ground beside him and moved around the tree for his first shot. He stepped into the bow, bringing it to full draw, took his aim and let the arrow fly. Before the first found its mark, he was nocking the second. When the arrow took the seated Apache in the chest, he straightened up, and fell forward on his face, yet before he hit the ground the second arrow was on its way. The whisper of the black missile cut between the trees and impaled the lookout to the ground as it penetrated his back.

The two horses of the lookouts, now free of their tethers, backed away from the man that had held them but began cropping at some bunchgrass that was too tempting to pass. Tate stepped back into cover, unstrung his bow and slipped it into its sheath, mounted up, and rode around the knob, taking an arroyo to the river bottom. He came from the junipers where the river bent back upon itself and pushed Shady into the water to cross the river. Once back on dry ground, both horse and wolf shook free of the wet and Tate readied himself by slipping the Colt from the holster. He looked to Lobo, "Alright boy, let's stampede those horses!"

He dug heels into Shady's ribs, and the big horse leaped forward, taking the bend around the point of the knoll at a run. Tate shouted, and Lobo charged with a growl and teeth bared. As if they were connected on a rope, all the horses and mules jumped as one and fought each other to flee from the wolf and screaming man. Laying low on Shady's neck, Tate looked through the flying mane, spotting the three Apache near the river as they scrambled for their horses. He was upon them just as a distant boom told of his men starting the fight. One of the raiders stumbled and fell on his face as the other two looked from Tate to the ridge and frantically took to their horses. Tate came near and dropped one of the Apache with a blast from his .44 caliber Colt, knocking the man off just as he mounted. The other man screamed and charged toward Tate with an arrow nocked and drawing his bow. He guided his horse with leg pressure and was almost upon Tate when the Colt bucked again, and red blossomed on the man's chest, arrow flying askew.

Tate heard two more blasts from a big buffalo gun and knew Johnson and his partner were taking their toll. The horses ran before Tate, no longer tempted by the graze or water, seeking only escape from the melee. He and Lobo herded the animals as if they had been in charge of the remuda all along, and as they neared the crossing of the Pecos, he hung back to let the animals slow and to wait for the other men. Within moments, he heard the muted thunder of hooves and knew the men were coming on the run. When they saw Tate, leaning on his pommel and Shady with his sides heaving, they reined up beside him.

"We got 'em!" shouted Johnson. "Boy, that was sumpin'!" he declared. "Me'n Taggert here got two of 'em, but I only winged the other'n 'fore he high-tailed it downriver!"

"That's not good," said Tate. "Their village is downstream, an' he's liable to get some more warriors to come after us."

He looked at the other men, "Everybody alright?" he asked, looking from man to man.

With four heads nodding, Tate reined around, "Let's get back to the wagons 'fore the rest of 'em come. Maybe we'll have enough to discourage 'em, but losin' seven men like they done, they might want a payback."

CHAPTER SIX
SANTA FE

JOHN BERNARD HAD KEPT THE WAGONS MOVING AFTER TATE, AND THE men left, and it wasn't until dusk when the remuda caught up with the train. They had just passed the crest and made the dog-leg turn back to the southwest when John sighted the dust cloud from the herd and turned back to check on the men. Tate rode up grinning, Lobo alongside, and John answered with his own smile, "Looks like you done alright!" he called as they neared one another. They had pushed the herd as hard as they would go just to catch up and all were relieved to be reunited with the others. Both wagons and herd had passed the battlefield and saw the remains of many horses and mules, broken and burnt bits of wagons, and other refuse from the war. The flocks of turkey buzzards took flight at their passing but soon returned to the remaining carrion. The stench was stifling, and they hurried past, eager to get over the pass.

"Well, we got 'em back, anyhow," explained Tate, "and didn't lose any men in the doin' of it. But we might still be in for some trouble." Tate stepped down and was joined by Bernard as they sought a seat on a flat boulder. He explained about the fight and the Apache losing seven men and high-tailing it for their rancheria. "I don't rightly know how many's at their village, cuz I just saw the smoke from their lodges.

But if they was to come after us, it would be with the knowin' of how many we have because that one that got away was part of the group that saw the wagons. So, if they come, I'm purty certain they'll come in force. But, if we're lucky, they'll reconsider and not come at all, you know, save themselves for an easier bunch of pilgrims or something."

"Well, not that I'd wish that bunch on anybody else, but I'd just as soon we get to Santa Fe without havin' to get in another fight," surmised John.

"I ain't hankerin' for another'n either!" added Tate. Both men slid from the rock, and watching the herd settle in behind the wagons, mounted up and went to the lead of the wagons. They were still less than a full day from Santa Fe, but too far to travel with tired teams, so John located a camp in the shadow of the timber covered mountains and drew up for the night.

TATE WRINKLED his nose at the typical smells of the cities, or what some would call civilization. Santa Fe was unimpressive with many of the buildings of adobe interspersed with an occasional storefront of wood. The streets were narrow and dirty, and the walkways were a combination of covered boardwalks and paths of dirt. Peasants and peons in dirty muslin clothing with rope sandals walked the streets, hocking their goods to any passersby. Bernard told him of a chapel that might give a little guidance at finding a family for the youngsters, and he made his way to the ancient landmark.

San Miguel Chapel stood behind a low wall, and its adobe walls rose above the surrounding buildings with its stucco-covered bell tower that stood open to the heavens. Tate slipped from his saddle and ground tied Shady, giving Lobo a sign to stay with the horse. He pushed open the broad, double door to a dim interior. His first step in on the clay tiled floor brought the attention of a brown-frocked friar who turned with a smile and extended his hand, "Buenos Dias, señor!" with a slightly raised eyebrow that betrayed his recognition of Tate as a visitor to their city. He continued, "How may I help you, señor?"

"Well, Padre, I have a slight problem. You see, I found a Comanchero that had bought a couple of youngsters from the Comanche, so I got them from him, and they're without a family and a home. I was wonderin' if you might help me find a good family that would like to have 'em."

"I see, what you have done is a good thing. How old are the children?" asked the priest.

Tate began explaining all about the siblings and their journey from captivity and through the mountains with the freighters. As he concluded, the padre said, "I might know of just the couple. The man is white, and his wife is Spanish, they lost their only daughter several years ago when the Comanche raided the city. They have the trading post on the square, the oldest one in town. They are good people, and Juanita has confided in me that she would like to have children, but Felix thinks they might be too old, but they are not. Maybe to have children of their own, but not to take in youngsters like those you spoke of, señor."

"Would you speak to 'em for me, Padre? I've got to go find Colonel Carson and let him know I'm here. I can check back a little later, if'n you don't mind." The padre agreed, and Tate excused himself, mounted up, and started for the northeast quarter of the town and Fort Marcy. Located on a low summit of a flat-topped hill, the massive walls of the fort stood as a bastion overlooking the city. With walls nine feet high and five feet thick, the fort had a commanding presence. Standing outside the fort were an adobe blockhouse and a powder magazine, keeping the explosives away from the main structure. The gates stood open, but Tate was stopped by a sentry who challenged him. Tate looked at the man and said, "I'm looking for Colonel Carson, where might I find him?"

"Who's looking for him?" growled the sentry, looking at Tate as if he was lice infected.

"I'm his new scout. He sent for me a while back, and I've just gotten into town. Could you direct me to him?"

"You'll probably find him at the boarding house, down thataway," he pointed with the muzzle of his rifle. "It's a two-story adobe with big windows and a wide porch. Most of the officers are billeted there. If he ain't there, he's probably at Mama Ortega's eatery, just down from there."

"Thank you, my friend," answered Tate and reined around to go to the boarding house.

It was easy to find, and Tate stepped down to tie off Shady at the hitchrail, and as he turned, he heard a familiar voice, "Well, it's about time! I was beginning to think you weren't coming!" Stepping from the shadows on the porch was the easily recognized figure of Kit Carson. His hand was outstretched as he came down the steps and the two friends clasped in a two-handed shake as they greeted one another. Two more dissimilar figures would be hard to find. Tate stood just over six feet tall with broad shoulders while the top of Carson's head barely came to Tate's chin, and if he stood behind Tate, he would not be seen with his thin frame. But what he lacked in size he made up in deportment. Piercing eyes with a flash of mischief, a broad and sincere smile showed loyalty and commitment, characteristics he was well known for, but his stamina and durability, never in question, was only known by those that served with him.

"Come in, come in! I'll have the boy look after your horse!" declared Carson, but as he turned, Tate snapped his fingers to bring Lobo to his side, and Carson looked down, "See ya still got that wolf, well, bring him on in, but I might have to introduce him to the widow Wanamaker." He stepped to the door and ushered the two through and followed close behind, "We've got a lot to talk about. By the way, did you come in by yourself?"

"No, I came with Bernard's freighters, thought it'd be safer with a train."

"You're right about that! There's been trouble a'plenty, from both the Confederates and the Indians. But we'll get into that later, let me show you to your room and introduce you around."

As they passed from the foyer into the sitting room, Tate admired the large home and looked at the heavy and dark wood furnishings.

The drapes at the windows were a heavy brocade that allowed little light to pass, but with large windows, the room was well lit. A uniformed officer sat on a settee as a woman poured tea in the cups on the tray on the table before him. The officer, a captain, stood when Carson entered, "Colonel, you're just in time for morning tea!" The woman turned with a smile and stood erect, teapot in hand with her other hand over the lid.

"So, Colonel Carson, is this the man you've been expecting?" she asked.

"Yes, Mrs. Wannamaker." He turned to Tate, "This is Mrs. Wannamaker, Tate. And ma'am, this is Tate Saint."

Tate had doffed his hat to show disheveled hair, but he smiled broadly and nodded his head to the woman. "Pleased to meet you, ma'am."

She looked at him with a pleasant smile but obviously noting his appearance, and he looked down at his buckskins, and back to her, "I hope you'll pardon my appearance, but I've just traveled many dusty miles to get here and I am looking forward to getting cleaned up a mite."

"That's perfectly understandable, Mr. Saint, and if you would like I'll have Jefferson draw you a bath. But what is that beast at your feet?"

Tate looked to Lobo, who leaned against his leg, "Oh, this is Lobo, my friend of many years." He let his hand drop to the scruff of the wolf's neck and said to him, "Lobo, meet Mrs. Wannamaker." The wolf stepped forward and sniffed the outstretched hand of the woman, then turned to look at Tate and returned to his side, dropping on his haunches. "Looks like you've made a friend, ma'am."

She smiled and nodded, then asked, "The bath?"

"That would be fine, Ma'am, but I have some other business to attend to first. But as soon as I return, I'll certainly take you up on that offer." He looked to Kit, "There is a little matter I do have to get settled. Has to do with a couple youngsters I took off a Comanchero. Survivors of a wagon train taken by the Comanche. The padre said he might know of a couple that would like to have a couple young'uns, so, I'm goin' back to talk to them."

Carson smiled, "Always lookin' after someone, aren't you? Alright then, but you'll be back for supper?"

"You bet." He turned to the woman, "And I am certainly looking forward to that home cooked meal, yes I am."

WHILE TATE MET WITH CARSON, the wagons had been taken to the big warehouse at the edge of town where Bernard kept his stores and Tate caught up with them there. He went to the cook wagon and found the youngsters. He explained about the padre and the couple he recommended, and the children listened attentively. "Now, I want to take you to meet 'em, and give you a chance to get acquainted. If you don't feel comfortable and don't want to stay, then you don't have to, and we'll keep lookin', understand?"

"Yes, but we'd rather stay with you, Tate," answered Ezra, looking at his sister nodding her head.

"Well, that would be fine, if I lived here with my wife and all, but I'll be going out with the soldiers and won't be around. And out in the wilderness fighting Indians is no place for two youngsters!"

"We know, but still . . ." he started, then asked, "Are these good people?"

"The padre says they are, but I haven't met 'em either. They own a trading post on the square and have lived here a long time. He said they lost their little girl to the Comanche many years ago, so, they have a place in their heart that maybe you two could fill."

Ezra looked at his big-eyed little sister and back to Tate, "Alright. Let's go."

Tate had them change to their other new set of clothes, washed them off a little and combed their hair as best he could, then walked together with them to the trading post. The Padre saw them coming and opened the door to greet them.

Tate was impressed with the couple, they were about his age and the man seemed to be a sturdy sort, well kept, average size, and friendly sincere smile. The woman was a petite-figured, long-haired somewhat distinguished type that surprised Tate as she immediately went to her knees to greet the youngsters and started talking with them, smiling all the while, and radiating happiness. She hugged Maribel tightly and embraced Ezra as well, then stood to look at her husband, her hands resting on the youngster's shoulders. "I want to take them and show them the place where they will be staying." It was more a declaration than asking permission and she turned to lead the children to the back of the store. They happily followed and turned but once to wave to Tate.

Tate looked to the padre, "That looks like a match!"

"I think so," he answered, then looked to Felix with a questioning expression. The storekeeper grinned and nodded, "They seem to be fine children. I haven't seen Juanita this happy in a long time."

Tate shook Felix's hand, "I'll be around a while. I'm staying at the boarding house where the officers of the fort stay, so if I'm needed, you can find me there." He turned to the padre, "Thank you," and shook his hand as he turned to leave. He took one last glance toward the back of the store, then to Felix, he said, "Tell 'em I'll come back 'fore I leave." Felix nodded and lifted his hand to wave as Tate stepped through the door.

CHAPTER SEVEN
ORDERS

"I just can't figger him out! One day he's fumin' and spittin' on how much he hates the Apache an' the Navajo, an' the next he's workin' on gettin' the go-ahead to establish a reservation for 'em. He got the idea from Beale, that navy officer that tried to take over California, who laid out a reservation near Fort Tejon for some of the tame Indians in California. He set 'em up proper to make farmers out of 'em. So now, Carleton wants to do that here with the Apache and the Navajo. That ain't what I signed up for, not that I'm ag'in it, but we were s'posed to be fightin' the Confederates!" declared an exasperated Carson.

The two men sat on the porch of the rooming house, sipping their coffee after the fine evening meal prepared by the widow Wannamaker, who prided herself on tending to the colonel's needs. Although she knew Carson was devoted to his wife, Josefa, who was pregnant with their sixth child and awaited the return of her husband to their home in Taos. The widow still waited on the colonel as if he was the only guest in her rooming house. She stepped through the door with the coffee pot in hand, "Would either of you gentlemen care for a warm-up?"

"Why thank you, Mrs. Wannamaker, that would be fine indeed," answered Carson, always gracious and mannerly. She filled his cup, offered the same to Tate who accepted, and she hustled back into the house, leaving the men to their talk.

Tate looked to his friend, "Didn't you fellas send the boys in grey back to Texas?"

Carson chuckled, "Well, that's the way we like to tell it, but truth be told, they whupped us at Valverde and at Glorieta Pass. It's only cuz we cut their supply lines, and the Indians stole most of their horses that caused 'em to tuck tail an' run." He took a sip of the hot coffee, leaned forward toward Tate, "Now, Carleton's got it in his head we're only s'posed to be fightin' Indians!" He leaned back, thoughtful for a moment, "The blasted redskins have been takin' advantage of all the white men fightin' each other, and they've been runnin' amok. Ain't a day goes by we don't get at least one report of a ranch or wagons gettin' hit and folks kilt."

"So, if you're not fightin' the Confederates, what am I doin' here?" asked Tate.

Carson looked to Tate, lowered his eyes to his coffee, and began, "I saw this comin' and I cogitated 'bout it for a spell. That's when I sent for you, and I also sent for a mutual friend. You remember Kaniache?"

"Yeah, he's that Ute war leader, ain't he? You mean he's comin' down here to help you?"

Carson nodded his head, grinning, "He's the one. If there was anybody that hates both the Navajo and the Apache, it's the Utes, Kaniache especially."

"But I still don't get what you're aimin' at. Just what is it you plan to do?" asked Tate, somewhat confused.

"I think General Carleton had his mind set on makin' a big name for himself. After he took Tucson then marched his California regiment up here, he had grand visions of his future. But since the war is no longer his playground, he's makin' himself a new sandbox. When he left here, he went down to an area that he fancied, called Bosque Redondo. He started layin' out his plan for a reservation and a nearby fort. He and his friend, General Sumner, have big plans for that fort.

Now, Carleton, he thinks he can do like they did in California and make farmers outta these Apache and Navajo." He shook his head, "But he's got another think a comin' on that!"

"Why's that?" asked Tate, leaning forward to hear the details.

"These natives ain't like those we knew up north. The Arapaho, Cheyenne, Sioux, Shoshone, and other plains Indians think different. You know how the big thing for a warrior is to count coup, take scalps, and gain honors in battle?" he watched at Tate nodded his head in understanding, "Well, the Apache, and the Navajo somewhat, think different. The one that has greater honor is not the great warrior, but the best thief!"

Tate scowled as he looked at Carson, "Thief?"

"That's right. Ya' see, a good thief can steal sheep, cattle, horses, and other plunder that keeps his family well provided for, but the women can't eat scalps, coups, or those things. So, they like the man that can go out and steal whatever they need to keep 'em happy." He chuckled as he thought of it, "Oh, the men like fightin' as much as any of 'em, and they're better'n most, but the fightin' is just so they can steal stuff, you know, like the cattle or sheep or horses."

Tate thought about it for a moment, then looking at Carson, "On the way out here, just over Glorieta Pass, we were hit by some Apache. But they didn't attack the wagons, they just snuck up behind us and stole the remuda!"

"But, knowin' you, you went an' got it back, didn'tcha?" grinned Carson. To which Tate grinned and nodded his head. "That's what I mean. They won't attack unless they greatly outnumber their foe and are reasonably assured of a victory. And when you see a couple of 'em trying to look peaceable or whatever, all they're doin' is checkin' you out to see what you have that they can steal, and how well armed you and your friends might be and if they can overpower you."

Tate shook his head, thinking about what he just learned, sipped at the last of his coffee and threw out the dregs over the rail of the porch. Carson did the same, then pulled out a sheaf of paper from his jacket pocket, extended it to Tate. "Read this."

Tate unfolded the letter to Carson. He looked at the signature and saw it was from of General James Henry Carleton. He skimmed over the first couple of paragraphs that had the customary greetings and questions about family. He also gave a report about the progress of the fort, told of his friend's death, and that the fort would be named in his honor, Fort Sumner. Then the next paragraph began with,

You are to command the garrison of Fort Marcy and start to the south toward our location. We have had reports of Indian raids by both Mescalero and Navajo that tally over 20,000 head of livestock stolen, over one hundred lives taken (Both Hispanic and Anglo), and the financial toll exceeds $225,000. You are to pursue the Mescalero to whatever lengths you find necessary. All Indian men of that tribe are to be killed, whenever and wherever you find them. If they come to you with a flag of truce, you are to say you have been sent to punish them for their treachery and their crimes. That you have no power to make peace, that you are there to kill them wherever you can find them. The women and children will not be harmed, but you will take them prisoners and feed them at Fort Stanton until you receive other instructions.

You are to show the Mescalero no quarter. They must be brought to their brutal senses without delay. I want the entire tribe to be incarcerated in Bosque Redondo before winter.

Tate stopped reading, astounded by the orders and looked to Carson, "This is what he expects?"

"That's right. He thinks I need to take all four companies from here and sweep the entire territory and round up every last Mescalero," answered Carson, "so, now you see why I need you to do the scoutin' for me."

"That's a mighty tall order, Colonel," answered Tate, handing the letter back to his friend.

"Yes, it is. But I've always done things my own way, so I'll just handle things as they come. Wherever and whenever I find 'em, I'll play my cards as they're dealt."

"And where and when are you going to start this dance?" asked Tate.

"The where is gonna be determined by you and me after we sit down and look over all the recent reports of raids and such. The when? Well, I'm hopin' we can head out in a couple days or so, dependin' on what we come up with."

"How long you think this little round-up's gonna take?"

"Hard to say, a month or two, I reckon," answered the Colonel. "Why, you got plans?"

"You know me, I'd just as soon be back at my cabin with my horses an' son and mindin' my own business rather than runnin' around the desert with a bunch of soldiers."

Carson reached into his other pocket, "Speakin' of that, I've got a letter for you. Just came this afternoon an' I think it's from Maggie!"

Tate busted out in a broad smile and reached to take the letter from Carson and with a muttered, "Excuse me," tore it open and began to read. As he perused the letter, he smiled, chuckled, shook his head, muttered an exclamation, then looked up to his friend. "I didn't think I'd been gone that long. Sean's done got married, to a Sioux no less, and Maggie and Sadie have returned to the cabin in the Wind Rivers. Now she's wantin' to know when I'm comin' home!"

He looked to Carson, "Well?"

"Well, what?"

"When am I comin' home?"

Carson shook his head, laughing, "I reckon as soon as we get this little round-up, as you called it, over with. So, the sooner we get started, the sooner you can go home. But in the meantime, you might wanna send the little lady a letter, to let her know you're still kickin'."

Tate stood, started for the door, and looked back at the colonel, "I aim to do that right now. I'll get this mailed in the mornin' and we can get busy plannin' our little set-to."

CHAPTER EIGHT
PURSUIT

"See, it's like this. I don't blame the Apache or the Navajo for doin' what they do. After all, this was their land, even before the Mexicans came. But it was no different here than other places. When the white man comes, he wants to take everything for his own and pushes the Indians aside. But none of 'em, not the ones on the great plains, or up in the mountains, or these here, like being pushed off their lands." He paused, knowing Tate agreed and understood but felt the need to emphasize the difference between the people.

"So, they fight for their homes. But their way of fightin' is different than the white man and the Apache are the best at what they do. They strike with small groups, when and where least expected, and only when they've got a superior force. And just like in other places, there's some nonsense by some struttin' popinjay that lights the fire," extolled Carson, leaning back in his chair behind the desk.

Tate stood, looking out the office window, and turned to ask, "So, what stirred the Apache up?"

"Best I can tell, it was what they call the Bascom affair. You see, there was this eager lieutenant that thought he could wipe out the Apache single-handed. When some raidin' Coyotero Apache hit a ranch, stole the livestock and took a young boy; Bascom was sent to find and return the twelve-year-old. But he ran into some Chiricahua and didn't know the difference, so he got their leader name o' Cochise, to meet with him. Now, Cochise brought his brother, nephews, his wife and sons, to the meeting. That's when Cochise said he knew nothing of the raid, but that Lieutenant Bascom took 'em prisoner to try to force 'em to release the boy. But Cochise escaped, raided some freighters and killed some Mexicans, then captured three Americans. He offered to trade the Americans for his family, but Bascom wouldn't have it. So Cochise went on'a raidin' and killed his hostages an' left 'em for the soldiers to find. Later on, his brother and nephews were hanged by them soldiers. Ever since then, Cochise and others have been fightin' and raidin' ever' chance they get."

"Is that what has Carleton so riled up?" asked Tate.

"Well, there's more to it than that. Ya' see, when Carleton was comin' out here from California with his regiment, they got into it with Cochise, his father-in-law, Mangas Coloradas, and an up-and-coming medicine man name o' Geronimo. It was what they call the Battle of Apache Pass. And if it weren't for the cannon that Carleton's forces had, Cochise woulda wiped 'em out. But Carleton claimed the victory, even though they didn't capture a single Apache, but they did run 'em off. They killed about sixty of 'em and only lost three of their own, so I guess you could call it a victory."

"Are we gonna have to go against any of these?" asked Tate.

"I don't think so. They're usually down south of Apache Pass or into the big bend area. The Mescalero we're after are 'tween us an' Fort Sumner and Fort Stanton. But, ya' never can tell 'bout these 'Pache."

THEY STARED into the rising sun as they mounted the slow rise of Glorieta Pass. Carson rode at the front of the long column of two companies out of Fort Marcy, with his second in command, Major Hostettler, at his side. With over two hundred troops of cavalry or mounted rifles, the support group of eight wagons trailed the force.

Riding four abreast, the boys in blue were an impressive sight as they passed the buildings of the Rancho de la Glorieta, otherwise known as Pigeon's Ranch. Although the owner's name was Alexander Vallé, he had become known as Pigeon because of the way he often went running around with his elbows sticking out. And that was the sight they saw as they started past the outlying buildings. Carson looked to the major, "Notice anything different over there?" nodding his head in the direction of the compound.

The major stood in his stirrups, "You mean besides Pigeon running this way?"

"Yeah."

"I don't see the usual bunch of horses in the corrals," answered the major.

Carson reined up, waiting for Pigeon to come close, then leaning down towards the man who was winded and gasping for air, "Apache! Them thieving savages attacked us just 'fore dawn an' took all muh horses and those of muh guests! You're just in time to go get 'em back!" he declared, between breaths. He leaned down with hands on his knees and his sides heaving, then stood erect to look to Carson. "Wal, ain'tcha goin' after 'em?"

"We will, but first tell me 'bout the attack. How many, when, where'd they go?"

"Don't know 'xactly, prob'ly near a hunnert. An' like I said, just 'fore sunrise an' they went down canyon!" he proclaimed, pointing to the trail into the wide canyon below the high bluffs.

"Didja lose anyone?" asked Carson.

"Got two wounded, but they ain't bad. We got three or four o' them but they hauled 'em off."

Carson started to answer the man but caught movement out of the corner of his eye and looked to see his scout approaching at a canter and leaving some dust behind. That was unusual for Tate, and Carson knew there was something urgent that had Tate coming back in a hurry..

Tate slid to a stop, "We got an ambush waitin' down the trail a ways. Looks to be about a hundred Apache, all hunkered down in the rocks below the rim of the flat-top."

Carson swung his leg over the rump of his mount as he stepped to the ground, looked at Major Hostettler, "Join us, Major," and motioned for Tate to step down as well. The three men walked off to the side together and Carson asked Tate, "So, did you see any horses, I mean a herd of stolen ponies?"

"No, just a dust cloud further down the valley."

"Early this mornin' they stole all the horses from Pigeon here and took off down thataway. And with what you've just told me, I'm thinkin' that herd is the bait in the trap." He looked to Tate, "You know where they're located, any way of gettin' behind 'em?"

"Not to get any of your cavalry back there, but I can, an' maybe if you've got . . ."

"Ho, Longbow!" the greeting interrupted Tate but he responded to his well-known Indian moniker and turned to see a grinning Kaniache and another man standing beside him. The two friends greeted one another with clasped forearms and a slap on the shoulder.

"Kaniache! It is good to see my friend. It has been too long!" declared Tate.

The man turned, "This is my brother, Big Nose, who wants to fight the Apache and the Navajo!"

Kaniache turned to Carson, "Little Big Man, it is good to see you. I am glad to fight with you." Carson greeted his friend with the same handclasp then introduced the major. Carson looked to Tate, "Looks like you've got your two men!"

Tate grinned and turned back to Carson, "Then let's get us a plan!"

The five men found a seat on a couple boulders, and with animated discussion that included drawing diagrams in the dirt, they soon had a plan for their confrontation with the Apache.

THE COLONEL HAD the troopers dismount and water their horses, letting them take advantage of the spring grass and giving them a short break. Tate and the two Ute scouts, knowing the soldiers would be watched, slipped away and started back down the trail toward Santa Fe, to give the impression they were leaving. Then they would circle wide around through the black timber and once atop the broad mesa, they were to make their way to the chosen site for their own ambush. Allowing Tate and the scouts enough time to make headway, Carson mounted up the soldiers and started the trek toward the anticipated ambush.

The three men, each skilled in wilderness stealth, quietly took to the trees atop the long mesa that followed the trail below. The black timber provided cover, but Tate led them into the brush-covered arroyos for further protection against discovery. Their almost two hours of careful riding brought them nearer the point of the mesa that was their goal. Tate reined up in the trees and slipped from the saddle.

"My guess is their horses are guarded, in the arroyo yonder. The rest of 'ems below the bluff there," he nodded toward the point of the mesa that extended into the valley. "Let's take out the men with the horses, then we'll drop over the edge to make our play," whispered Tate, starting toward the end of the tree-lined gulley. As he guessed, they soon neared the gathering of mounts, guarded and held by five men. Tate and the two scouts were belly down as they looked under the low-hanging branches of a large juniper. The three men were similarly armed, bows with a quiver of arrows hanging from their belts, rifles slung over their backs, pistols in their belts, and the ever-present knives. With hand signals, Tate directed Kaniache and Big Nose to either side of the group and designated their targets. "I'll take mine first, but you be ready with yours." The two nodded and slipped away to take their positions.

The guards were complacent, two standing near the arroyo edge, the other three gathered in a group, talking and dozing. Typical of those left behind, all were young warriors and probably unproven. Tate crawled through the junipers, keeping well covered and sliding his longbow beside him, although he knew it was useless from a prone position, but his confidence was in his ability to reach the man, unheeded. Within moments, he was behind the one guard on the edge of the arroyo. The man leaned on his lance, head down, probably snoozing and expecting nothing. Tate slipped his Bowie from its sheath and slowly rose behind the piñon. He took a deep breath and with two long strides, he was behind the man with one hand over his mouth and drawing the razor-sharp Bowie across his throat. The man's lance started to fall, and Tate grabbed at it as he lowered the guard to the ground, blood covering his arm. He stepped back to the piñon, used a handful of needles and dirt to wipe his arm clean, then picked up his longbow for his next target.

The second guard was on the opposite side of the arroyo and partially shielded by a scraggly juniper. Tate looked to his left, over the edge of the arroyo to check the other three that were still seated together, paying little attention to anything but their conversation. Tate stepped back from the edge, out of sight of the group of guards, and as he moved to the end of the branches of the juniper, he brought the bow to full draw with the arrow nocked and held with the finger of his left hand. He brought the tip in line with his target, who was seated on a rock beside the tree, and let the arrow fly. It whispered to its mark, burying itself in the man's chest, but the cry of the man as he fell backwards startled the other guards. But as they rose from their seats to look, arrows from the bows of Kaniache and his brother dropped the first two, and Kaniache's second arrow impaled itself in the neck of the last guard before any of them could sound an alarm.

As agreed, they scattered the mounts and together started to the edge of the bluff. They bellied down to crawl unseen to the edge and Tate pointed out where the Apache probably were lying in wait. He pointed to a notch for Big Nose to use to drop over the edge, another for Kaniache, and indicated where he would descend. "Once everything starts, use your bows first so the rest won't know we're above them, but as soon as you're discovered, then open up with your rifles. And move around, so they think there's more!" With a nod, each man slipped away to make his descent and take his position.

CHAPTER NINE
AMBUSH

"That's the point, up there," exclaimed Carson. "Are you sure you wanna lead that bunch up the hill?" he asked Major Hostettler.

"Absolutely, Sir!" declared the enthusiastic major. He had seen little real action against the Confederates, and he was anxious to be 'blooded' in battle. He was a good horseman and had insisted he lead the charge with Sergeant Upshaw and his chosen platoon. "We can do it!" he added.

"Alright then, spread the word to the others to use the wagons for cover, and you hold back until it starts," instructed the cColonel.

The major reined around and started to the back of the column. Carson motioned for a lieutenant to come forward, "As we planned, hold the column up until the wagons come forward then keep the troops on the downhill side. Just around that point up there is where we expect the Apache."

"Yessir!" declared the lieutenant and he held up his hand and hollered, "Column, halt!

Off an' on!" he ordered, a familiar command the troopers understood to be 'Off the horses and on the ground.' The men swung down and stretched their legs beside their horses as they waited for the wagons. In short order, the eight wagons were stretched out on the trail and the men remounted, moving in a four-abreast column, although it was not easy going in the rough ground beside the trail.

The colonel, a lieutenant, and the first sergeant with the bugler, rode at the head of the column. Carson wanted the first part of the column to be seen before the wagons and they were well ahead of the rest of the force. He knew the usual attack by the Apache would come after most of the men had passed the point with the assault coming at the rear of the line, making it difficult for the soldiers to turn around and face the battle. Carson made it a point to have those nearby to keep their eyes on the trail and not be looking for the attackers.

Moving at a regular pace, the dust was minimal but the progress seemingly slow. When expecting something to happen, time seems to stand still, and the nervousness was showing. Some of the men had seen little, if any, Indian fighting and each had his own internal battle to keep from breaking ranks and running.

BIG NOSE HAD EASILY DESCENDED through the scrub piñon and taken his place among a cluster of limestone boulders at the edge of the long talus slope. Kaniache had a more difficult time making his way down a steeper drop-off, as his position was above the middle of the line of attackers. But he carefully picked his way to a large sandstone rock, sufficient for cover. Tate's position was at the edge of a cluster of juniper and farther from the attackers, but his skill with the longbow and the range of his Spencer still gave him an advantage.

When the column came in to sight, Tate waited, hand on the scruff of Lobo's neck, unconsciously rubbing his hand over his mane and behind the wolf's ears, as he watched for the first wagon to show around the point of the mesa. He had marked his first targets, two Apache hunkered down behind some large boulders near the bottom of the talus slope, but above the others. When the wagon showed, he let fly the first arrow to find its mark in the neck of the Apache seated at the highest point of the slope. The Indian slumped forward, grabbing at the arrow, but no sound was made. Kaniache was to take his cue from Tate's action and Big Nose take his from Kaniache. Within seconds, both Ute sent arrows into their chosen targets. The first few moments saw three Apache slump in death. The three men took aim on their second targets and two of the three scored a killing hit, but Big Nose's arrow hit the rock in front of his man, causing the Apache shout an alarm. But the others had already loosed their barrage on the wagons and the man's warning was drowned out with the rattle of rifle-fire and the second arrow from the Ute found its mark.

Three more arrows whispered their way to their marks, but this time Kaniache's man moved and shouted a warning to the others. That was the cue for the three attackers to move and start using their rifles. The big Spencer roared, and the blast echoed across the notch where Tate sat concealed, but the leaden missile brought down another Apache. He jacked another cartridge into the chamber, cocked the hammer, but was startled when a warrior sprang from in front of him, screaming his war cry, tomahawk raised as he leapt from the rock. Before Tate could bring his rifle up, the grey wolf sprung from his place and caught the Mescalero warrior in mid-flight, sinking his teeth in the man's arm and bearing him to the ground. Wide eyed, the Apache squirmed, but not quick enough as Lobo's teeth were buried in his neck and the wolf shook his massive head side to side, ripping the throat from the man whose death throes splattered blood on the nearby rocks. "Thanks boy," muttered Tate as he leaned back from the boulder, looking at his friend.

With the rifles sounding behind and above them, and the soldiers taking cover behind the wagons, the Apache soon realized their attack had been thwarted, but there was no ready route of escape. The scattered band continued to send volley after volley into the wagons until the screaming charge with the bugle blaring came thundering through the trees, with Major Hostettler leading and waving his sabre in the air and he shouted to his men.

The last thing the Mescalero expected was for the mounted Cavalry to attempt to charge into their fire, but the wall of mounted soldiers in blue caused many of the warriors to jump from their barricades and run for cover further up the slope. But each time one rose from behind his rocks, the three scouts would fire upon them, turning them to run downhill toward the trail.

When Carson saw the warriors fleeing from the charge and the rifle fire above them, he shouted orders, "Lieutenant! Take a platoon and head them 'pache's off!" he waved in the direction of the fleeing warriors. With their horses atop the mesa, and their way of escape blocked by Tate and company, and the charge coming from the major and his men, the warriors only route to flee was down the slope toward the trail. Lieutenant Whitcomb shouted his orders, "Second Platoon! On me! Pistols at the ready!" and as soon as the men approached, he took off, sabre in hand yelling, "Chaaarrrge!"

Carson's pride swelled as he watched his men file by, lying low on their horses' necks, following the daring lieutenant as they charged toward the rag-tag bunch of Apache running through the sage and cacti, trying to escape what was supposed to be their victorious attack. "Go get 'em boy!" yelled the colonel as he pulled his horse near the wagon.

Tate and the Ute scouts kept up their three-man barrage, moving between shots, confusing the fleeing Apache. The contour of the land in the basin where Tate had stationed himself drew some of the warriors to try to make it to the top and to their horses by way of the slope above Tate's position. He had just fired a shot and was moving in a crouch to another cluster of rocks, when he came face to face with another Apache. Both men stopped, Tate knowing that he had jacked another cartridge, but now slipped his thumb on the hammer to bring it to a cock but did not move. Suddenly the Indian, rifle in his left hand, reached for his belted pistol as he started toward Tate, but Tate brought up the butt of the Spencer and savagely hit the man, smashing his ear and cheekbone, knocking him to the side. As the Indian fell, he pulled his pistol to try to shoot his assailant, but Tate had brought the rifle to full cock when he swung at the man, and now lowered the muzzle toward the staggering warrior and pulled the trigger. The big blast of the Spencer knocked the man to the ground as the .56-56 caliber slug tore through his torso, leaving a hole the size of Tate's fist as it exited his back.

Tate's attention was captured when he heard the bugle sounding the charge and he looked below to see the irregular formation of cavalrymen fighting their way through the scrubby piñon and juniper, pursuing the fleeing Apache. Suddenly, they were confronted by a narrow arroyo, but the men and horses never hesitated and each in turn jumped the narrow defile and kept up the chase. With their Springfields bouncing in the narrow scabbards that hung just behind their right leg, muzzles down, the men used their pistols, carefully rationing the six bullets. But it was obvious some had already emptied their pistols and had holstered them, grabbing at their rifles to use the loaded weapon, but when empty, to use as a club. But none of the men hesitated in the charge and some even mimicked the Rebel yell as they pursued their quarry.

Tate grinned, proud of the men as they kept their seats even over the rough terrain. He looked further down and saw the men in the charge along the lower trail, those led by the tow-headed lieutenant who had lost his hat, his blonde locks flying, but he pointed his sabre as they charged. Within seconds, they overtook the first of the fleeing Mescalero and swung around in front of the band, shooting those that lifted their own weapons toward the soldiers. The skirmish was short-lived as several of the Apache raised their hands, still holding their rifles, over their heads and stopped running. As Tate watched, the lieutenant moved his men into a semi-circle to round up the raiders and with hand signals made the warriors drop their weapons.

With another look around at the barricades formerly manned by the Mescalero, Tate signaled to Kaniache and Big Nose to return to the mesa top and retrieve their horses. Climbing back up the rugged slope was a bit more difficult, but when they topped out, they looked at one another, grinning and breathing heavily. Tate noticed both men had fresh scalps hanging from their belts, but he made no mention of them. With Lobo at his side, he led the other men back to their horses.

Before mounting, each man checked the loads of his rifle and pistol, re-armed, and stepped aboard. Tate had spotted a notch they could negotiate to make it to the bottom and the trail, which they used to re-join Carson and his troopers. The colonel was smiling broadly when the three men rode up, "Now, that was a fight!" declared Carson, watching the three men dismount. "Come on over here, I've had our cook get us some coffee goin' an' it should be about ready!"

As they dropped to the ground, the cook brought cups and poured hot coffee for each of the men. Carson looked to Tate, "We've got about forty prisoners, but we'll drop them off at Fort Union, then we'll go on to their village."

Tate looked at his friend, dropped his eyes to his cup, remembering the colonel's orders were to 'kill every man, and show no quarter. Only the women and children were to be taken, prisoner.' But he also knew Kit and knew he was determined to do it his own way. He had never been comfortable with the orders from General Carleton, but he was willing to subdue the Mescalero, but not kill them indiscriminately. That was madness.

CHAPTER TEN
VILLAGE

"MAJOR, YOU TAKE SECOND PLATOON, B COMPANY, AND ESCORT these prisoners to Fort Union. We'll be going south to their village, and if we take more captives, I'll send Lieutenant Whitcomb to join up with your troops and deliver them as well. Now, after we leave that village, we'll head west. We've had reports of raids on some ranches there, and you can meet up with us in that area. Understood?" asked Carson.

"Yessir. But what if Union doesn't want the captives?" asked the major.

Carson chuckled, "You tell that Major Periwinkle or whatever his name is that you have orders from General Carleton. That whippersnapper ducked out of the fight at Glorieta, and he's probably never seen an Apache, so it'll be a good experience for that pup!"

The major ducked his head as he tried to stifle a laugh, then looked up to Carson, smiling and said, "It'll be my pleasure, sir! Also, what about burying the dead?"

"I'll leave that up to you. If you want the captives to do that, or if you want to have your troops handle it. The Apache are not as particular as other tribes, they usually just wrap 'em up and stick 'em in a hole, maybe with some ashes or pollen. But, some of 'em don't like handling the dead, afraid of their spirits or something."

"We'll handle it, sir," answered the major, snapping a salute to the colonel and turning on his heels to begin his assigned task.

Carson turned to Tate, "Alright then, you an' your scouts take a looksee at that village, and we'll come along shortly."

Tate nodded and turned away, signaling Kaniache and Big Nose, and within moments the three were on the trail. Once they rounded the last point of the flat-top mesa, they took to the red-dirt flats that paralleled the Pecos River to the south. He aimed for the notch at the west end of the long finger ridge that pointed to the river for their route to the top. Familiar country to Tate, since he led the group to retrieve the stolen horses from the freighter train of Bernard, he knew they could come on the village from the west mesa and have a good promontory to scan the entire rancheria.

They crossed the long finger ridge and worked their way, using the many arroyos and scattered timber for cover, to the edge of the flats that overlooked the valley of the Pecos. They tethered their mounts and crawled to the edge to scan the valley. Surprised by the size of the rancheria, having about seventy wickiups, Tate knew this was a prominent location and might have been home to more than the warriors they already encountered. He slipped his scope forward, and with a patch of buckskin wrapped over the end to prevent any reflection, he scanned the entire area. The village straddled the winding Pecos with wickiups on both sides, most using the willows, alders, and cottonwoods for shelter and shade. Women worked on hides, fixing meals, tending to children, and older children scampered about involved in the usual games of young natives. It was an idyllic scene of family life, but the men were missing. A few white-haired elders sat by their woven willow wickiups, probably sharing memories and war stories with one another, but Tate could see no warriors.

He pointed out two gulches that came from the east side into the valley, marking them as possible entries to the valley for the troops. Noting another wide arroyo that came from behind their promontory and widened as it emptied into the valley, he briefly explained to the Utes his plan. They quickly slid back, rose to a crouch, and returned to their horses. They hastened on their return to give their report to Carson.

When they reached the trail just before the Pecos crossing, they met the column led by Carson, and with the men taking a brief break, Tate and Kaniache explained their strategy to the colonel. "And you say you didn't see any other warriors?" he asked.

"Only old men, women, and children. But the size of the village made me think there had to be more warriors than those we tangled with," explained Tate, shaking his head. He had just drawn a map of the plan in the dirt at their feet and looked up to Carson.

"And how many lodges?" quizzed the Colonel.

"I calculated about seventy," answered Tate.

"Yeah, that would mean, oh, 'bout thirty or so more warriors than what we got," surmised Carson. "An' you think we can get to the village 'fore they hightail it?"

"If you wanna take the long way around that big mesa to the east, you would have a better approach for a surprise, but that'd take you more'n a day outta your way," explained Tate. "But you know as well as I do that they could have scouts out and already know you're headed their way. That's just the way it is with them 'pache."

"Alright, but if we push it a little, we can still get 'em 'fore dusk. So," and he nodded to the two officers sitting nearby, "I'm gonna have those boys take First and Second Platoons, A Company and Kaniache and Big Nose can take them to these two spots," he pointed at the diagram in the dirt, "and I'll bring First Platoon, B Company and come with you to this spot." He looked to Lieutenants Whitcomb and Barrett, "You two wait, for my signal. I'll have Tate signal his scouts and pass it to you. I want all three of us to enter the valley at the same time, we don't want any of the Mescalero escaping. Understood?"

The two eager officers answered in unison, "Yessir!"

"Lieutenant Whitcomb, you're senior officer and company commander, so you're responsible!" added Carson.

"Yessir, understood, sir!"

"And send me a messenger, I need to send a dispatch to Hostettler."

"Right away, sir," replied Whitcomb, turning away to fetch a man to be the colonel's messenger.

Carson looked to Tate, "As I think about it, if we take as many captives as it sounds like, I might as well have them all sent to Fort Sumner and General Carleton. I'm sure he's gettin' anxious to put his big plans for his reservation into practice."

"Sounds reasonable," agreed Tate. Then at a motion from Carson, he rose and summoned Kaniache and Big Nose to get ready to lead out. They would split the force at the crossing of the Pecos, Tate taking the colonel's troop straight south through the red-dirt flats and follow the same route he and the scouts used earlier. Kaniache and his brother would lead the rest of the troop parallel to the Pecos but farther east, in the rolling hills below the high-topped ridge that rose to a ragged-edged mesa.

It was a hot afternoon, the dried grasses crackled under the horses' hoofs, their shod feet kicking at the rocks, and dust rising like a brown mist to cover both man and beast. The creak of leather from the saddles and the rattle of canteens were the only sounds of life until the column reached the notch at the tail of the long finger ridge. Here they had to climb the slope, and the muttered complaints of the troops muffled the other sounds. Once atop the ridge, they could see for many miles north and south and the thin blue lines of cookfire smoke marked the location of the rancheria.

"We'll move down into that long dry wash for a little cover, that leads to the valley yonder." He pointed to the west edge of the valley, and the wide mouth of the arroyo showed as a scar on the sharp edge of the mesa. "That's where you'll enter the valley, 'bout in the middle of the village. I'm goin' out on that point," nodding to the jutting edge of the valley wall, "and scope it out in case some o' them missin' warriors are back," explained Tate. Carson nodded his agreement and with the typical hand signal, motioned the column forward.

Tate slipped away and worked toward the chosen promontory. He bellied down and scanned the valley and the village but saw nothing out of the ordinary. Satisfied, he started to crab back when a low growl from Lobo stopped him. Coming toward the village from the downstream end was a band of warriors, returning to their village, driving some cattle and horses, undoubtedly the spoils of their raid. Tate put the scope on the band, calculated about forty warriors, then quickly went to his horse to catch up to Carson and give the warning.

"Is there any way we can get word to the other side?" asked Carson upon hearing Tate's report of the additional warriors.

"No sir, not in time."

"Then we'll just have to proceed with the plan. We still have 'em outnumbered by a considerable margin, it just might be a little more of a fight. So be it!" he declared and motioned the column forward. Tate started toward the chosen point for his observation and signal to the other side, while Carson led the troops in the shallow depression toward the head of the arroyo that he would use for his approach to the village. Once Tate was in position, he watched as the warriors were welcomed back and was relieved to see the focus of attention was on the men and their spoils. Some of the young men began driving the cattle to the meadow area above the village, and Tate used his scope to locate the other two platoons on the northeast side. Both were in position, and Tate used the agreed upon signal, using a hand-held polished disc similar to that used in the new heliographs, and utilized the reflection from the hot afternoon sun to signal Carson. He watched with his scope to be certain the signal was received, and with a wave from Carson, he saw the troop begin its approach down the dry arroyo. The wash widened as it neared the valley and Carson's plan was to approach with a broad front and stretch that front even wider as they entered.

Tate gave them a couple moments to make the needed progress, then turned back to signal the other two platoons. Their movement told Tate they had received the signal and he, with Lobo alongside, sought a better position in the event his help was needed in the coming conflict. He had no sooner slipped and slid down the slope from the mesa-top to find his cover behind a cluster of basalt rocks when the excitement began.

The activity suddenly increased with several people running and shouting the warnings, pointing to the troops that showed themselves at the mouth of the wide arroyo. Without hesitation, warriors started shooting, taking cover behind the many wickiups, shouting warnings and orders to one another. The colonel ordered the bugler to sound the charge. At the clarion call of the bugle, the men responded, rifles blasting, before they slipped them back into the scabbards and drew their pistols. The men charged into the village, weaving in and out among the canopied lodges, firing at anyone that appeared to be a threat, ever mindful of the command from the colonel, 'Women and children are to be taken captive!'

With the sudden appearance of more troops from the south end of the village and even more from the upstream end, the villagers were stymied from every direction and sought shelter in the frail, round wickiups. Rifle fire sounded, echoing back from the valley walls, screams from women, war cries from men, whinnying from terrified horses, and crying from frightened babies, made a cacophony of sound that heightened the confusion. Tate saw a handful of women, dragging children behind them, trying to escape upstream, weaving in and out among the willows, and he put a shot just in front of the leading woman to get her attention. The woman instantly stopped and looked in his direction, and visibly resigned herself to their fate. She dropped to the ground, pulling her child to her lap, and the two hugged one another as did the others. Tate looked back to the battle, heard the gunfire lessening and saw Carson approaching a man whose hands were uplifted, holding a rifle over his head.

When Carson saw one man, barking orders to the others and looking around, he marked the man as one of the leaders, and watched as the man stepped out from behind a wickiup, also holding his rifle over his head as he approached. Carson slipped his sabre back into the scabbard at his side, then nudged his horse toward the man. He was a dignified sort just a touch of grey in his hair that showed from beneath the wide headband, long, loose hair hanging to his shoulders. His visage was wrinkled, but determination and confidence showed in his eyes. He was deep-chested, and his legs bulged with muscles that showed on either side of his long breech-cloth, and he spoke English clearly. "I am Caballero, chief of this rancheria. These are my people." He looked at Carson and around at the other men, now holding their pistols on the other warriors, "You have more men and better arms. We are at your mercy."

Carson stepped down and faced the man, and stood of equal height to the chief, something he was not accustomed to, since he only stood about five feet eight inches himself. He spoke simply to the leader, "I have been given orders that we are to kill all the Mescalero men," and he watched as the man's eyes widened and anger flared, "I have even been told to tell you that we are here to punish you for your many raids and murders of white people and that all your men are to be killed. Even if you came with a flag of truce, I am ordered to kill. But," and he paused as he looked at the man, "I will not do that, for I believe that to be nothing more than madness. My chief, General Carleton, has established a reservation for the Apache at Bosque Redondo," and Carson noted the man's recognition of the name, "and you and your people are to be taken there. You can take what you can carry, but you will not have horses or cattle, and your village and stores will be destroyed. The general wants the Apache people to become like the Tiwa and Pueblo people and be farmers and raise your own food."

The man had listened carefully to Carson before responding, "The land of Bosque Redondo is a good land. We have camped there many times. But to be farmers is not in the nature of the T'nde people. We are not like the Tiwa or the Navajo to dig in the dirt like animals."

Carson paused a moment as he looked at the man, feeling some compassion for him as he knew this was the same as a death sentence to this proud people, but he continued, "This morning, many of your warriors crossed over to the other side when they tried to ambush us.

This many died," he flashed both hands of fingers six times. "Would you want me to send these warriors with them?" he motioned to the other men gathered behind the chief.

The chief hung his head at the news of the failed ambush. Carson had rightly guessed the man was hoping his other warriors would come to their rescue, but this news was devastating to him. He lifted his eyes to the colonel, "No. We will go. We have no other choice."

"Good. Have your people gather what they can, and my men will torch the lodges."

CHAPTER ELEVEN
RANCHES

FEAR AND HATRED WERE WRITTEN ON THE FACES OF ALL THE Mescalero as they watched the soldiers put the torch to their wickiups. They were allowed to take what they could carry, but most of their winter stores, extra clothing, and blankets were destroyed. At the last minute, Carson relented and allowed enough horses to be kept to transport the people, and all their weapons had been confiscated and put in the wagons. As the colonel, standing with Tate and the two lieutenants, watched the torching, a courier arrived from General Carleton. Carson quickly read the message and looked up to Tate and the others, "Looks like we've been ordered to Fort Stanton. But on the way, we're to keep up the fight with the Mescalero. The general wants all the Mescalero on the reservation in a month's time." He folded the orders, shaking his head, and put the folded paper in an inside pocket of his jacket.

Carson looked to the junior officers, "Lieutenant Whitcomb, you and your platoon will stay here until Major Hostettler arrives with his captives. Then both of you will go south to Fort Sumner, deliver the Apache, then come due west and meet up with us at the foot of Manzano Peak. I'll have Big Nose stay with you as your scout."

"Yessir. And sir? How long should I wait for Major Hostettler?" asked the lieutenant.

"No more than two days. If you have to pull out before he gets here, send a courier back to let him know."

"Yessir!" answered Whitcomb snapping a salute to the colonel.

Carson turned to Tate, "We're headin' south southwest through those flattops. And if I remember right, there's a wide valley that takes us right through, but there's very little cover. So, you and Kaniache need to keep your eyes open."

"I understand, Colonel," answered Tate, and with a nod to Kaniache, the two scouts started on their way. It was late afternoon and they were riding into the setting sun. Tate retraced their route to the village, taking the mesa trail to the south end of the long finger ridge, then turned to the south and the mouth of the wide valley that would lead them away from the scene of their brief battle. The sun hung on the horizon of the shadowy flat-tops as they rode into the wide valley. Everywhere there was sage, greasewood, cacti, and bunchgrass, but little water. Tate had expected no less, but there was a dim trail, probably a path traveled by Apache between rancherias, but not a regularly traveled hunting trail. Although the desert had mule deer, a few desert bighorns, plenty of jackrabbits, but little else. They found a cut-back in the shoulder of the mesa on the north and chose that as the site for the camp this night. Then Tate looked to Kaniache, "I think I'll do a little scoutin' by moonlight, wanna join me?"

"That would be wise. This night has a big moon and would be a good time for a raid," answered the Ute, somberly. Tate wasn't sure if he meant a good time for the Apache to raid their camp, or for the two of them to raid the camp of the Apache. No matter, the scout was necessary, and he preferred the night.

When the meal was finished and the soldiers were going to their blankets, Tate and Kaniache left the slumbering men behind them as they silently slipped from the camp, bound to the west and a better scout of their trail. As they rode, Kaniache asked, "Have you had the wolf long?"

"Since he was a pup. He's gettin' old, but he ain't slowin' down any. Guess it's the easy life he's had with me."

"The wolf is a spirit animal to the Apache. When they see one in the night, they believe it is the spirit of one of their enemies come for revenge."

"Interestin', maybe we'll let that spirit put a little fear in 'em, if we get the chance."

"The man he killed on the hill in that first fight had more than a little fear!" chuckled the Ute, remembering the attack by Lobo when he took down the charging Apache.

"We have another'n back at the cabin. My son takes him. He's one of the pups from this'n, so he's a mite younger and a bit bigger, but he's midnight black!"

"Aiieee, to have a black wolf attack you in the night!" replied Kaniache, shaking his head at the thought.

Tate reined up, held up his hand for Kaniache to stop, then looked at him, "Do you smell smoke?"

"Yes, but it is too much for a campfire. It must be a village or more," whispered the Ute.

They moved into the shadow of the bluff and slipped to the ground. Both men chose their bows as their weapons of stealth and Tate led the way as he walked to the end of the shoulder that shielded them from the view of the extended valley. They moved at a crouch and went to the edge of the shoulder to look beyond. Even in the moonlit night, the smoke that rose from the valley floor pointed to the unimaginable scene. What had once been a prosperous ranch with many buildings and even an adobe wall, now lay in ruins and piles of burnt timbers. Little flickers of flame peeked between burned boards to show the fire had not consumed everything. Tate searched the nearby flats for any movement, anything to show the presence of the attackers, but there was none. No evidence of any life. Even the carrion eaters had yet to receive their invitation or else they avoided the smoldering ruins, afraid of fire. Both men waited several minutes, watching, and still nothing moved.

Even the night predators like the coyotes and night hawks were absent.

Finally satisfied there were no attackers remaining, the men retrieved their mounts and Tate sent Lobo to scout ahead. Within a few moments, they rode upon the ruins. Within the walls of the courtyard, four bodies were sprawled, naked, and mutilated. One woman and three men, scattered, with some body parts removed and tossed aside. Tate rode closer to what had apparently been the main house, now a large pile of ashes within crumbled adobe walls. He stepped down, ground tied Shady, and picked his way into the ruins. He put a handkerchief over his nose as he caught the stench of burned flesh, soon seeing the partial remains of at least three children and two more women.

Back in the courtyard, he went to the skeleton of the barn or stable, but without stepping in, he could tell there were at least two more bodies of men and several carcasses of horses. Tate was surprised to see the remains of the horses, as the Apache would most often take the animals, but the barn was probably ablaze before they breached the walls. A corral was attached to the barn, but it was empty. He turned to see Kaniache approaching, "The Apache killed everyone. I do not think they took any captives, there is no sign."

"I agree. This was just to take any cattle or horses, weapons, and destroy what they left," answered Tate, shaking his head. He looked around, saw the small frame that covered what was probably the well and went to get some water, but Kaniache stopped him.

"No drink. Bodies in well," he said simply.

Tate looked around, saw a water trough to the side of the remains of the bunkhouse, and led Shady to get a drink. There was nothing but some ashes floating, so he skimmed them off with his cupped hands, and brought some of the water to his mouth as Shady buried his nose in the cool water. Kaniache copied Tate and let his horse drink his fill. Once the horses stepped back, Lobo lapped until satisfied. "This won't be enough for the troops, reckon we'll have to find some elsewhere," observed Tate.

They pushed on to the west but a few miles further, the valley split with an island mesa standing as a sentinel at the crossroads. Tate chose the route to the south and after another four or five miles, they came across another decimated ranch. Although there were not as many dead, everything had been destroyed and all the stock had been taken, leaving everyone including the women and children dead and mutilated or burned. The well had also been a dumping place for at least two bodies. Tate looked to Kaniache, "Are they just on a raid, taking livestock and killing people, or are they leaving us a trail?"

Kaniache considered the question, "It is a large band, more than five times two hands. It could be they want to drive out all those that are not Apache."

"Carson said the chief of that bunch they captured was a fella name o' Caballero. He said that chief was married to a daughter of the chief known as Mangas Coloradas and that Mangas and Cochise fought in that Apache Pass Battle and they're determined to chase all Americans out of Apache territory. Now, if this is his bunch, they're sure doin' what they set out to do."

"They know the soldiers are on their trail. They will set an ambush."

"I'm thinkin' you're right about that. Tell you what, you wait here for the colonel and his boys, I'll head out that way an' see if I can find us some water. They're gonna need it to cross that wasteland we're comin' to, I reckon."

It was well after midnight when Lobo came trotting back to Tate. He stepped down to greet the wolf, and as he stroked the beast's head, he felt water on his muzzle. Tate grinned and chuckled, "I knew you could do it boy." He stepped back up to his saddle, and spoke, "Take us to it, boy." The wolf turned and trotted back the way he came. Rising out of the dry valley, Lobo led his friend up a notch to the wide expanse of flats, covered with scattered juniper and piñon. A dim trail wound through the trees and cacti, past a stretch of nothing but cacti and bunch grass and into a swale that held a tank of slightly brackish water. It was not uncommon to find the occasional depression, known as a tank, that caught and held any rainwater and seepage, runoff when there was any, and held the water as it slowly evaporated in the hot desert sun. But they were fortunate, this was a sizable tank and held enough water to give relief to the thirsty animals. Tate let Shady have his drink, then took a couple handfuls for himself, sloshed it around his mouth and spat it out. He shook his head, *Don't taste very good, but it'll serve its purpose.*

He led Shady back to a cluster of juniper, stripped the gear and tethered him within reach of some gramma and stretched out for a snooze. He needed some rest before the troops caught up with him, then he'd have to find the raiders, and that was going to be a challenge.

CHAPTER TWELVE
AMBUSH

THE COLD WET NOSE OF LOBO ON TATE'S NECK BROUGHT HIM instantly awake, but he did not move, and barely opened his eyes to search for any reason for alarm. Lobo was bellied down beside him but watched Tate as he looked around. It was still dark, but the stars were snuffing their lanterns and the moon lay low against the horizon. Tate guessed it be approaching four, maybe a little later. He slowly sat up, looked to Lobo as the wolf was pacing toward where Shady was tethered and back to Tate, obviously telling him to follow. Tate trusted Lobo more than anyone and when he had cause for concern, Tate's only choice was to heed the wolf. Within moments, he had Shady rigged and he stepped in the stirrup, speaking softly, "Alright boy, lead the way."

Lobo took off at a run and Tate kicked Shady to a canter to try to keep the grey streak in sight in the diminishing darkness. They dipped through a dry arroyo, weaving in and out of the scattered juniper and piñon, and took a long slope that stretched across a wide saddle and ended on the round point of a high mesa. Lobo stopped, turned to Tate, and waited as the man dismounted and tethered Shady. Then he led the way as they slowly approached the edge of the mesa, bellied down, and stopped above the rimrock. Tate had his scope, but it was still too dark to make out whatever was in the bottom. Lobo looked at the man, stretched out with his muzzle between his paws and relaxed.

"Now what is this all about? You could've gone to sleep back where we were near that tank, but no, you had to come here." Tate spoke in barely more than a whisper, but soon followed the example of his wolf and crossed his arms, lay his head down and waited for the slow rising sun to bring a little light.

When darkness slowly lifted her skirts to show the thin line of blue grey silhouetting the eastern horizon, Tate had found a better position and was seated behind a low boulder. He looked at the terrain, about four hundred feet below the mesa top where the valley stretched to the south but not before another wide arroyo joined it at the base of Tate's mesa. Still too dark to use his scope, he scanned the wide valley and its fork for any sign of movement, but he saw none. He leaned back and chose to use this time for his customary early morning conversation with his Lord. He was thinking about his family and asking God to watch over them and smiled at the memory of good times at the cabin. It was warming to know Maggie and Sadie waited for him, and as he thought of Sean and his new wife, he shook his head, grinning at the thought. But he was brought from his reverie by a low growl from Lobo.

Tate looked at the wolf, saw he was looking at the canyon of the fork, and he swung his attention to the dry wash. With the splash of sunlight as old Sol made his appearance, Tate saw a long line of riders moving to the mouth of the canyon. He lifted the scope and scanned. At least sixty Apache warriors rode silently on the sandy bottomed arroyo, led by an unusually large man whose feet hung below the belly of his horse. The leader was deep-chested, broad shouldered, and with muscular legs and arms. He wore only a breechcloth and tall moccasins, a headband, and a rifle suspended from a sling at his back. Tate was certain this was the notorious Mangas Coloradas, always described as the biggest Apache of them all, and the cruelest raider and fighter, determined to rid all of Apache country of Mexicans and Whites.

They stopped well back from the junction of the two canyons, dismounted, and sent six or seven of the warriors to take the horses back up the draw. Using hand signals, the leader split the force, with warriors divided on both sides of the valley. Tate watched as the men scattered, each finding his own position. As he scanned with the scope, Tate was astounded at the way the Apache moved and seemed to melt into the terrain. One moment he saw them, and the next there was no movement, no give away, no evidence there had ever been anyone there.

He lifted his scope to look back up the wide canyon, searching for the troops, but the many flat tops obscured his view of the valley once it bent back to the east. He did see a slow rising dust cloud, caught in the bent rays of the bright morning sunlight. He knew the troops would be coming down this wide canyon, right into the waiting ambush. He guessed they were still two, maybe three miles away, but would be here all too soon. Twisting around to get a better look at the hidden Apache, he heard the sound of horses below him and he scurried to the edge on his left to see the Apache's herd gathered in the depression that resembled a box canyon just below his promontory.

He returned to his first outlook and scanned the valley bottom, searching for the waiting Mescalero. With his practiced eye and thorough search, he began to make out several of the warriors, those that were using bunchgrass and greasewood as their cover. From the canyon bottom, they would not be seen, but from high above, he could make them out. The Apache were well-known for their ability to hide in plain sight, and Tate saw how simple and true that was, for many of them could only be made out after careful scrutiny. Some had thrown a blanket over themselves, tossed dirt atop the cover, and now faded into the terrain. Others stood motionless behind the dead trunk of a juniper or twisted cedar, some crouched behind sage, while others could only be made out by the black of their hair, but even that would be camouflaged with twigs.

As he examined the terrain, trying to decipher what the Apache would do and what Carson's response would be, he looked for possible cover or escape routes. But as he considered it from the viewpoint of the soldiers, he guessed they would not be looking for an attack from these sparse slopes. Just beyond were several rocky ridges or escarpments and talus slopes, all that would provide good cover for attackers, and just the place where the soldiers would be expecting an attack. But at the junction of the canyons, there was no reason to expect an attack and the soldiers would be lax and inattentive, just enough that the first volley from the ambush would be devastating.

Tate looked again at the slow-moving cloud of dust that marked the approach of the soldiers, knowing he would have to warn them, somehow. He crabbed back from the edge, Lobo at his heels, and returned to where Shady was tethered. He slipped the Spencer from the scabbard and hung it across his back with the rawhide sling. The longbow came easily from its sheath, and he lifted the quiver of arrows from its tie by the cantle. He returned to his first promontory, looked again at the progress of the column, and strung his bow. His longbow, standing just over six feet and made of strong yew wood, had a draw weight of over one hundred fifty pounds, more than what most men could pull. But Tate had long ago mastered 'stepping into' the bow instead of drawing it with one arm. He pulled three of his long black arrows from the quiver, sticking two into the loose soil at his feet, and nocked the third. He had marked his target, the middle of the dry creek bottom where the soldiers would travel, then stepped into his bow, keeping his right hand that held the nock near his ear, and pushed his full weight against the bow. Angling the arrow slightly up, he let it fly and watched as it arched across the valley bottom and bent its trajectory to the dry creek bed, impaling itself in the far edge. Tate smiled, guessing it was a distance of over three hundred fifty yards, which would be five or six times further than the useful range of a typical Apache bow. Two more arrows flew silently overhead, each striking a little closer back towards Tate, found their mark, effectively giving a three-arrow warning to anyone that came up the canyon. He was hopeful that either Kaniache or Carson would recognize his arrows as a warning.

He dropped his bow and using his scope, he again scanned the bottom, looking for any alarm among the attackers, but there was no movement, anywhere. He had to double check to make sure they were still there, but his hopes were dashed as he spotted first one, then another, and more. He considered using his bow to see if he could take out a few of the attackers without giving away his location, but he thought it best to wait for the column. He looked back to the valley floor and was surprised to see Kaniache, standing beside his horse and looking at the arrows. He had arrived so soon after, Tate thought it even possible he saw the arrows strike. He watched the man through his scope, and saw he was looking back at the angle of the arrows, trying to determine where they were shot from, and Tate quickly withdrew his small reflector and used the rising sun to send the beam back to the Ute. Instantly the scout remounted and took off at a run toward the troops. Tate smiled, knowing his warning had served its purpose.

Tate looked again at the waiting Apache and with no movement detected, he thought maybe he had not been spotted. He started to rise and the sudden tensing of Lobo, made him spin on his heel to see two charging Mescalero warriors. They were shocked at the lunge of Lobo, and that hesitation gave Tate the edge. He grabbed at his Bowie at his back and with one very practiced movement, he brought the big knife over his head and sent it flying into the first attacker, who looked down at the elkhorn handle protruding from his chest and slowly crumpled to the ground, falling on his face and driving the hilt of the knife to his chest. Lobo had knocked the other warrior to his back and in one swirling movement, locked his teeth on the man's throat, stifling his cry and breaking his neck. Tate looked around as he nocked an arrow, searching for any other attackers and seeing none, he snapped his fingers to bring Lobo to his side. He reached down and rubbed behind his ears, "Good boy, good boy!"

Together they made a quick check of their mesa top with a short walk near the edge, but there were no others to be seen, and Tate knew when the first two did not return, more would be sent. Back at his original point, Tate looked to the valley to see the column. Lifting his scope, he saw Kaniache riding beside Carson, and the soldiers were now in an eight-man front, which meant they were readying a charge. But Tate knew they would not know the location of the ambush and would need to be warned again. He waited till the column showed itself nearer the junction, then he slipped the Spencer from the sling, and on one knee, took aim at one of the warriors nearer the front of the ambuscade, one that stood behind the twisted, dead cedar. He fired his first round and the big boom of the Spencer echoed across the two canyons, sounding like three or four rifle shots. He quickly jacked another cartridge, pulled the hammer to full cock and took aim again. His first target had fallen, and when the Spencer boomed again, another warrior, crouched behind some greasewood, rose up and fell forward. It took two more shots before Tate got the response he was trying for, and several of the warriors from below began returning his fire, giving away their location.

Carson wheeled the troops and had the bugler sound the charge and instead of an eight-man front, three ranks of sixteen took the lead and charged at the now exposed Apache. Rifle fire sounded like a barrage of canon in the narrow defile between the mesas. Screaming of warriors, shouted orders of officers, shouts of soldiers, and cries of the wounded caused a cacophony of terror that filled the entire canyon.

Tate quickly sheathed the bow and Spencer, swung aboard Shady and with Lobo at his side, they took the edge of the mesa at a notch above the gathered Apache horse herd. Leaning back against his cantle, he stretched so far back his shoulders almost touched Shady's rump and the grulla dug his hooves in and hunched down the steep slope. The sudden appearance of the man and the wolf startled the herd, and when he hollered and waved his hat, they took off at a run. Two warriors jumped to their feet and grabbed for their weapons but were stopped by the bark of Tate's Colt and red blossomed on their chests. Before they fell to the ground, Tate was past them, and another warrior was drawing a bead on the man, but Lobo knocked the

Apache to his back, causing his rifle to clatter down the rocks. Lobo didn't stop and kept close behind Shady. Before the others could react, the horses had stampeded down the wide arroyo and Tate, Lobo, and herd were out of sight.

The rifle fire and screams from the battle spooked the horses even more, and they scattered among the fighters, trampling several warriors in their panicked flight. Tate was now in the midst of the fight, and he soon emptied his Colt, jammed it back in the holster, and grabbed his tomahawk, swinging at any standing warrior as he passed. He split the head of the first, swiped off the ear of another, and buried the blade of the hawk in another's neck, causing him to have to heave with all his strength to free the buried hawk. He goaded Shady on and within moments, he was behind the line of the soldiers, and reined up to let the boys in blue have their way with the Apache.

CHAPTER THIRTEEN
AFTERMATH

"Bugler! Sound Recall!" ordered Carson, pulling on the reins of his excited mount, backing away from the conflict. The battle had raged incessantly for several minutes, although it seemed like hours to the combatants. The Mescalero fought as they screamed their war cries, wielding their war clubs, hatchets, knives, and, when possible, their bows and arrows. Several had rifles, but only a few were breech loaders, and the Indians were limited on their ammunition. Others with muzzleloaders, had already given up on reloading and used the rifles as clubs. The troopers rode their horses over the carcasses of many, knocking others down and trampling on them. With most of the men armed with two pistols, they fired indiscriminately into the melee, killing and wounding several. Tate saw a few of the men, apparently having emptied their pistols, now wielded sabers or used their pistols as clubs. With all the focus on the conflict, no one noticed the handful of Mescalero that grabbed at the horses and swung aboard to escape during the battle.

With the sound of the bugle, the men in blue pulled back, but the battle was over, and the only warriors that remained were those dead and dying. It was a gruesome scene on the slight rise that before had shown only greasewood, sagebrush, bunch grass and a scattered few juniper and piñon, but now the ground was torn and dug with the marks of horses. Instead of living things, contorted and bloodied bodies lay scattered as a mown harvest over freshly plowed ground. As the men gathered together, horses still fidgety and prancing, they tried to control the animals, but most averted their eyes from the horrific sight. Carson wheeled his horse to face them, "Alright men, you've fought well. Dismount and reload your weapons, tend to your horses, and we'll take care of the wounded." He looked to Lieutenant Barrett, "Form a detail as soon as they're ready and retrieve any dead and wounded of ours. I want a head count as soon as possible!"

Carson looked to Tate, motioned him near, "Did you find any water?"

"Yessir, and if these Mescalero hadn't interrupted my sleep, I'd still be snoozin' beside that tank. It's about three miles from here," and he nodded toward the butte, "atop that big plateau yonder."

The sun was nearing its zenith when the troops finally started from the scene of the battle. They had buried three of their men, had three more bandaged but mounted, and caved in a rocky escarpment over the bodies of thirty-two Apache. Kaniache read the sign of the escapees and reported there were at least a dozen, including the leader that Tate thought was Mangas Coloradas.

The men breathed heavy as they mounted and formed the column, riding side by side in the column of twos. Tate found a notch that gave access to the plateau top, and the sun showed little mercy on the tired men. The tank of water shone its welcome in the bright sunlight, but the stagnant water was taken of begrudgingly. The horses, instead of drinking deep and long, satiated their thirst and stepped back from the green water with scum floating at the edges. The men tried to push away the scum and bring handfuls of drinkable water to their mouths. Some splashed their faces and necks for any relief, but none were smiling. Mumbling and complaining was common. But all knew they were fortunate to have even this water in such a dry and desolate land.

"Kit, I think it'd be wise if we stayed here, got a little sleep in the shade of those trees yonder, and didn't try that," nodding toward the wide, brown flat that stretched beyond their view, "until after dark. It'll be a little cooler, horses won't tire as easily, and, well, you know all that. So, what say?"

"I think you're right, Tate." He motioned the lieutenant over, "Have the men take to the trees, get a little sleep. No fires till closer to sundown. We'll be travelin' by night for a spell."

"Yessir," responded the anxious junior officer. He spun on his heels and started toward the men, speaking to each one and repeating the orders of the colonel.

Tate looked to Carson, grinning, "You kinda enjoy havin' these youngsters snap to every time you bark, don't you?"

Carson let a smile paint his face as he dropped his eyes, "You know, Tate. All my life, I've been smaller than most other men and had to fight 'em or prove myself in some way before they'd accept me as an equal. And yes," and he looked up to Tate who stood almost a head taller, "I do get a kick outta havin' 'em jump when I bark!" The two friends chuckled as they led their mounts toward the trees to find themselves a bit of shade for a little rest.

THE WANING, three-quarter moon hung from the dark underneath of the black cloud, the only cloud in the star-bedecked sky. Tate and Kaniache had left once full dark hung over the wide plateau and the rest of the troops were rigging up to follow. The two scouts rode together as they let their mounts have their heads and pick their own way through the cacti strewn flats. Tate lifted his head at the distant wail of a lonesome coyote and grinned when an answering cry came from nearby. Lobo had stopped and listened, looking for the answering mischief-maker of the desert. But his hesitation was short-lived, and he trotted on, leading the way. They didn't expect to discover anything or anyone in the middle of the desolate flats, except maybe a few more coyotes or jackrabbits, but even the rattlesnakes found cover during the night hours.

When they judged it to be about midnight, they dismounted and walked, leading their mounts with loosened girths to give them a little relief. After a short distance, they used Tate's floppy felt hat to hold some water for the horses and took limited sips for themselves. Tate guessed they had made close to twenty miles, but also knew that was less than halfway across the dry flats. Once mounted, they split up to search for any sign of other travelers or perhaps some unexpected but hoped-for source of water.

When they came back together at the edge of a dry wash that scarred the flats, neither spoke, their facial expressions giving the expected and disappointing report. Once again, they dismounted and led their horses, down into the wash and clamoring up the other side, only to find a seat on some sandstone to give both man and horse some much-needed rest.

The troopers followed the same manner, dismounting and walking their horses. But every step of man or beast brought tufts of dust spiraling up like wispy brown snakes crawling up their pants legs. Several lifted their neckerchiefs over their mouths, but it was little help. Since there was no trail, the Colonel had the men moving four abreast and rotated the two platoons to take the lead. And even in the cooler night, sweat caught the dust and made mud balls at the corner of the eyes and the edges of mouths. They were allowed to untuck their blouses, but that just gave the powdery dust another avenue to sweat-soaked bodies and tears, and sweat made rivulets of mud down faces and chests.

But as the night wore on, the bodies were dry and mud cracked, chafing the skin and irritating men and horses alike. Once more, the order was passed to dismount and loosen the girths to walk the horses. Although the men grumbled, they knew they had to take care of the horses, for without them, they would not make it across the dry flats, and the buzzards would feast on their bones.

Suddenly, one of the horses shied and started bucking, the trooper trying to hold tight to the reins, but when he saw the big rattler, he jumped back away from the startled snake. Somehow the horse had stumbled upon the reptile and both were scared and reacted. The horse, now free of restraint, bucked away into the night, leaving the trooper shouting and whistling. He pulled his pistol, wanting to shoot the snake, but a barked order from the sergeant, "Holster that pistol! Whaddaya wanna do, tell every 'Pache the country where we are!" The sergeant tasked two men to climb on their horses and retrieve the mount, and the men quickly tightened the girths, mounted up, and went in pursuit of the horse. When they returned, leading the humbled horse, the others had stepped aboard and once relieved of the horse by the lone walker, they joined ranks.

As the rising sun warmed their backs, they could see the Manzanita Mountains in the distance. Although they still had many miles to go, the sight of tree covered mountains gave hope to the thirsty travelers. Canteens had long been emptied, and horses stumbled on the dusty flats, but heads were lifted higher than just moments before with the end of their path in view. Tate and Kaniache were sitting in the shade of some stunted cottonwoods when they sighted the dusty column, and Kaniache mounted up to lead them to the small pool of fresh spring water that lay in the shade of the trees. Within less than an hour, the exhausted men and horses had been refreshed and had found enough shade to crawl under and sleep.

CHAPTER FOURTEEN
DISCOVERY

LOBO ROLLED OVER ON HIS SIDE WITH HIS LEGS OUTSTRETCHED AS HE watched Tate move his scope left to right. Tate scanned the valley and arroyos below the timber-covered hilltop that served as his observation post. He and Kaniache had been tasked with a broad scout of the hills that shouldered up to the Manzanita Mountains. These were the tail end of the Sangre de Cristo mountain range that stretched from mid-Colorado Territory to central New Mexico Territory. It was in the Sangres that Tate built his first cabin and made his first home, but that was far to the north from where he now lay in Apache country. Although the ancient town of Albuquerque was only two days ride to the north, this land was the historic territory of the Apache. Several bands claimed this land: Mescalero, Lipan, Coyotero, Chiricahua. But their claim had been contested by the Spaniards and Mexicans and now by the White-eyes or Americans.

Yet, war leaders like Mangas Coloradas, Cochise, and the medicine man, Geronimo, were committed to driving all of them from their territory; however, their recent bloody raids were replacing peace and contentment with fear and hatred. But that was the goal of Mangas, to do whatever it would take to put fear into the hearts of all non-Apache, including the Navajos, and rid their land of all others.

Tate and Kaniache were searching for villages or rancherias of the Apache, but failing that, some sign of the raiders that had decimated the ranches and farms, and mutilated the families on those homes. Some of those ranches were built on old Spanish Land Grants that dated back as much as a hundred years and the families had worked hard to build a home, but the rise of the Apache and their migrating farther north had brought conflict and death. Tate saw no sign of life, much less a village. Earlier he had passed signs of prospecting and mining, but it appeared to have been abandoned, although not many days ago.

The foothills of the Manzanitas were a maze of valleys, arroyos, dry washes, hills, mesas, buttes, and more. As Tate looked, he thought how easy it would be to get lost in this massive kaleidoscope of timber. The black forests lay like blankets on each of the hilltops draping over the slopes and into the valleys, leaving little space for trails or villages. Spruce, fir, and pine held their greenery close and only offered low down views among the thick forest. Tate could see little from atop the round knob, except for the granite peaks that marked the crest of the Manzanitas that lay to his right. "There could be a couple thousand Apache in those trees, and I couldn't see 'em 'fore I stumbled over 'em." He didn't realize he had spoken out loud until Lobo lifted his head and looked at him with an expression that said, "What'd you say?"

"Sorry boy, just thinkin' out loud," added Tate, continuing his scan. He was also thinking about Kaniache and his scout to the north and west of the camping soldiers. The orders from General Carleton was to round up and bring in all the Mescalero, and to do it within the month. But the general was assuming they would be easily found and subdued and hadn't considered the other bands of the Mescalero that were further south. The vastness of the territory made the task almost impossible, but he respected Carson's determination to get the job done. The recent discoveries of the massacres at the ranches had raised the ire of the colonel, and with his already well-grounded dislike and distrust of the Jicarilla Apache whose country was in the southernmost part of Colorado Territory, his anger was building to hatred and was driving him to complete his assignment.

In the years Tate had known Carson, he always thought he had an understanding of the natives. Both men had married into the Arapaho, and Carson's second wife was of the Cheyenne people. But now married to Josefa, the daughter of a wealthy Mexican couple in Taos, his temperament did anything but mellow. Perhaps when at home with his family he could be sanguine, but here among the raging Apache, his mood had darkened, and he was becoming more and more intent on the capture or destruction of the raiders.

The thick timber stymied Tate's visual search, so he focused on any indication of smoke that would betray the location of a village. The bright sun that fought its way through the clouds, and the grey underbellies of the low hanging cumulus, made it difficult to spot grey smoke against the same colored clouds. Yet he scanned the trees, watching, waiting, for anything that might be a giveaway. Nothing.

He scooted back and put the scope into his saddlebags and swung aboard Shady. With slight knee pressure, they moved into the trees, Lobo leading the way. With no obvious trail, they zig-zagged through the woods, moving quietly on the bed of needles and the occasional patch of last fall's matted Aspen leaves. The groves of the white-barked quakies were light and fresh with the whispering breeze rattling the leaves of the close-growing trees. It was in the second cluster of Aspen where they crossed a recently used trail. Tate slipped to the ground to examine the tracks, noting the passing of many horses, most of them unshod ponies. The narrow trail only allowed a single file of riders, but the tracks were many and the soil recently disturbed. The trail pointed to the black forest at the base of the granite peaks, and Tate assumed that would be the location of their rancheria. *Makes sense,* he thought, *that country could hide several villages and provide good cover too.*

He led Shady into the thicker woods before he remounted. He looked down at Lobo, "Boy, you're gonna have to be real careful and watchful, this is mighty dangerous country, and I'm thinkin' there's quite a few fellas ridin' thataway that would like to take my scalp." With a nod, he motioned the wolf ahead, and carefully followed, keeping well into the trees. He knew it would be more difficult to follow the trail below from the deeper woods, but it was definitely safer.

In a short while, the trail below broke from the trees to cross a wide arroyo to disappear into the trees on the opposite side. But if Tate were to follow, he would have to leave the cover of the woods, and he had no idea what the other side held, knowing the warriors would quite often leave someone behind to watch the trail. He chose to move further uphill and wait to cross until there was ample cover. Within less than a mile, he found his crossing and was soon hidden in the thick timber on the far side. Throughout the rest of the afternoon, the story was repeated again and again, crossing after crossing, always requiring a go-around to stay out of sight.

The setting sun had silhouetted the granite peaks when Tate smelled smoke. He instantly reined up and dropped to the ground. After tethering Shady with a slip knot that could be freed if necessary, he slipped his longbow from the sheath and hung the quiver from his belt. With the bow strung and Lobo at his side, Tate gave a wave of his hand to send the wolf ahead. He knew Lobo would never reveal himself until given the signal from Tate but would search out any village or camp and wait for his man.

About five hundred yards from where he tethered Shady, Lobo had bellied down under the widespread branches of a tall spruce. The bed of needles was deep and soft, but Tate wasn't looking for comfort as he stretched out beside his friend. In a sizable basin, lying between shoulders of the foothill that stretched to the granite peak high above, lay the sought-for rancheria. Thin columns of wispy smoke from many cookfires twisted to the sky and were lost in the low hanging clouds. Tate surveyed the many wickiups, counting close to a hundred lodges. The people were busy, the usual family activities, yet Tate saw the break in the trees from which peeked a wide mountain meadow holding their horse herd. As he watched, he saw every lodge had at least one man, several with two or three. And with many women that saw themselves as warriors and often rode with the men on their raids, the village could field a force of perhaps two hundred fighters. Tate shook his head at the thought, yet watching the families, children playing, women cooking, all happily mixing together, it was hard to envision the barbarity and cruelty these people were capable of inflicting on others.

Suddenly Lobo snapped his head around and let a low growl come, but Tate put his hand on the wolf's neck, whispering, "Quiet boy." He had heard the same sound, the whisper of a pine bough brushing against cloth or leather, then the murmur of voices as the stealthy footsteps of at least two people moved behind them. Tate rolled to his side to look behind, seeing where Lobo searched the trees, and just beyond where they could see, they heard the footsteps and murmurs of two people. But Tate recognized the sounds, a woman and a man, probably trying to find a place of solitude for their rendezvous. He smiled at the thought of young love being the same everywhere men and women are found, but the last thing he wanted was for two lovers to sound the alarm of intruders. Tate knew they were well hidden, but he lay quiet and unmoving, waiting for the two to move on but they stopped.

For several minutes, all Tate could do was lie still and listen. The lovers were out of sight, but not out of earshot, and it was all he could do to keep from laughing out loud. He couldn't understand the words, Apache was dissimilar to the native languages he knew, but the tone and rejoinder were sufficient to know it was the same conversation heard time and again the world round. He rolled back to his belly to look to the village, and surveyed the scene again, memorizing the lay of the land and any possible locations for ingress and egress in case the colonel decided to attack.

As he looked, movement caught his eye, and he watched as a man, about the same age as him, move purposefully up the trail that led around the shoulder where Tate lay watching and went into the trees. Tate's brow furrowed as he thought, then hearing approaching footsteps with no intent at stealth, he realized that man was probably the father of the girl back in the woods. He shook his head and smiled at the thought, and he knew he had to wait to see what happened. He could only visualize the events by the sounds he heard, but he knew the father had found his quarry and he wasn't happy. After a few shouted remarks, Tate heard footsteps moving quickly through the trees toward his pine-needle bed, but they passed by, and Tate saw the moccasins moving at a run toward the camp. A few more loud remarks, and the other two, walking along the dim trail soon faded away and re-appeared on the path leading into the camp. The man had a firm grip on the young woman's arm, and she struggled but walked at the man's side with her head hanging.

Tate grinned, shook his head, and after a quick survey of his area, he and Lobo came from under the big spruce and were soon at the side of Shady. He knew they would have to find their way out of the dense woods with little help from the rising moon, for with the cloud cover as it was, little moonlight would be seen.

It was well after midnight when Tate led Shady to the edge of the camp to be challenged by the sentry, but the tired man was recognized, and after tending to his horse, he stumbled to his blankets and with Lobo at his side, drifted off to a few hours sleep.

CHAPTER FIFTEEN
WHEELED

CARSON AND TATE WERE ENJOYING A CUP OF STEAMING COFFEE, sitting near the fire in the cool of the morning. The sun was barely peering over the eastern horizon when Kaniache strode to the fire and poured himself a cup to join the two men. Carson broke the silence, "So, what'd you two fellas find in your round-about scout?"

"I found a village back in the thicker trees near the base of that first tall peak, over a hundred wickiups and, from the looks of things, over two hundred warriors," reported Tate, taking another swig of coffee.

"Anything else?" inquired Carson, looking across the fire at his friend.

"Saw some sign of abandoned diggings, looks like whoever it was left out in a hurry and recently. Other'n that, nothin' to speak of."

"How 'bout you, Kaniache?" asked the colonel, pouring himself some more coffee.

"Sign of raiding party, maybe twenty warriors. Maybe Mangas. Saw miners, this many," he held up six fingers, "big wagon." He extended the fingers of both hands, moved them together, "Meet Mangas soon."

"Did you warn 'em?" asked Carson, concern showing on his face.

"White man thinks all Indian alike, not believe," declared the Ute, emotionless.

Tate nodded his head, looked to Carson, "He's right about that. If he'd tried to warn 'em they probably woulda shot him 'fore he could say anything."

Carson looked to Tate and shook his head, "You're probably right. Sometimes I forget how stupid some people are, especially those that are blinded by greed for gold." He stood, pacing about, then looked to Tate, "Did that village show any sign of raiding parties, or anything like that?"

"No, only sign I saw was from a big bunch that I thought might be raiders, but when I scouted the camp, they were cuttin' up meat and passin' it around. Not very much at that. So, I think it was just a huntin' party."

Carson looked toward the distant mountains, then back down to Kaniache, "Where'd you see Mangas?"

The Ute picked up a stick and began to diagram in the dirt, showing his route and the trail of the Mescalero. His crude map showed the location to be west and slightly north of their camp and he said, "One hand ride." His description told of the time it took the sun to move the width of one hand across the sky, or the equivalent of about an hour.

Carson's decision was instantaneous, and he turned and shouted for Lieutenant Barrett. When the man trotted to the fire and saluted, Carson barked, "Have the troop ready to ride in ten minutes, extra ammo, leave the wagons with guards here. We're ridin' light and fast!"

"Yessir!" answered the officer and spun on his heel, shouting for the first sergeant, "Sergeant McIntosh!" As Tate watched, the sergeant stepped to, saluted, nodding his head at the orders and quickly turned to move among the men, sparing no words to get the men moving. He picked two volunteers to stay with the men and wagons that were to remain behind and in short order the troop was ready to ride.

It was the unmistakable stench of burning flesh that stopped Tate and Kaniache. They were still in the trees and had seen just a wisp of smoke, but this told another story. Tate spoke softly to Kaniache, "You go back and warn the colonel, I'll scout it out and will wait for you."

The Ute quickly reined around and started on their backtrail and Tate swung down, rifle in hand, and motioned Lobo to scout ahead. With Shady ground tied, he trotted behind Lobo, moccasins finding quiet footing in the pine needles.

At the break in the trees, Lobo had stopped, looking beyond and waiting for Tate. Once beside the wolf, Tate went to one knee and slowly and as quietly as possible, brought the Spencer to full cock. He searched the scene before him, the only thing moving were the thin wisps of smoke, a scrap of neckerchief snagged on the corner of the burnt wagon box, and a tuft of hair of the mane on a dead horse. But Tate watched and waited, slipping his own neckerchief over his mouth and nose to stay the stench. He recognized these as the miners described by Kaniache and the carnage told of their meeting with the Mescalero.

Satisfied there was no danger, Tate rose and slowly walked from the trees, looking at the story that was written in blood before him. Every man had been killed and mutilated, two had apparently shown themselves as good warriors for they were lying off to the side, stripped and mutilated but not scalped. The wagon had been tipped on its side and was mostly burned. Two men had been spread-eagled on wagon wheels, hung upside down, and fires had been put under their heads for the men to know what would happen and suffer not only the fear beforehand as the Apache reveled in the torture, but the actual horror of being burned alive. Their heads had burst, and the blackened corpses showed little from the neck up. One man had been staked over an anthill but only after strips of his skin had been peeled back, exposing the meat of his chest and shoulders, and with his eyelids cut off, he had watched the black and red ants cover his body, face and eyes as his life ebbed with the blood flowing from the wounds. It was a short while later when Tate found the body of the last man, who had apparently been drug back and forth behind a horse until his skin had been peeled off and his body left to bake in the sun.

Tate had finished his survey of the scene when he heard the approach of the column. He walked to the tree line and waited for the troop and held up his hand to stop them. "Colonel, it's a mess. Don't know if you want the men to see this."

"No, they need to know why we're huntin' these murderin' savages!" he vehemently declared. He knew what to expect, but once he rode upon the wagon, he also covered his face with a neckerchief and turned his head away. He barked at the lieutenant, "Get a burial detail and put these men in the ground!" He wheeled his horse around and went to Tate, now standing in the shade of a tall ponderosa. Slipping to the ground, "This mornin'?" he asked.

"Ummhumm, they ain't been gone more'n an hour or so," answered Tate, his words somewhat muffled by the scarf.

"Then let's get after 'em!" growled the colonel. He swung his mount around and went to the junior officer. "You leave these men to get this done an' catch up with us! We're goin' after 'em. So, don't let 'em get caught with their drawers down! Have Sergeant McIntosh take over an' you come on!"

"Yessir!" answered the young man, then turned to the sergeant to relay the orders, but the salty sergeant spoke first, "I heard 'im!"

THEY LEFT the troop at a full gallop. The trail made by the attackers was easily followed and it was evident they were not moving very fast. Kaniache looked to Tate, "They do not know or care they are followed."

"No, but I think they're headin' to that village I spotted yesterday. If they get there and have them join up with 'em, we'll have more trouble than we want! That village has 'bout two hundred warriors!" declared Tate. He held his hand up to signal Kaniache to slow, and as they dropped to a canter, Tate stood in his stirrups to try to see further ahead. They were approaching a good-sized, timber-covered hill and he motioned for them to take to the higher point. Once atop, they stepped down, tethered their animals, and looked for a good observation point.

From the cover of the thick spruce, they searched below and beyond, and it was Kaniache that pointed, "There!" In a slight basin with thinning timber, movement showed the presence of several horses. Tate leaned against the trunk of the tree to stabilize himself as he extended the scope for a better look. In the trees below, the Mescalero had stopped, dismounted, and were resting in the shade, letting their horses drink and graze. A small, spring-fed stream trickled at the edge of the clearing, and the men lounged about, some examining their plunder from the miners.

The two scouts quickly remounted and went to meet the troop. With their report to the colonel, the attack was planned, and the lieutenant was dispersed to move around the hill and come at the raiders from the other side, Carson would give him time and the attack would be coordinated by Tate atop the hill. His opening shot would begin the fray. Within a short while, Tate saw the movement in the trees and as he watched the Apache, he saw they heard the approach of the troops, but they only thought it was those coming from around the hill. When Tate saw they were near enough, he took aim with the big .56-.56 Spencer and squeezed off the shot. His target was knocked to the ground, but the blast of the big rifle startled all the warriors who were expecting an attack from the trees, not the hill. Tate jacked another cartridge, took aim, and squeezed off another shot, then scampered up and moved for his next round. By the time the troop mounted their charge through the trees and from the trail, the Apache were confused and taking cover in all the wrong places. The rattle of rifle fire bounced off the hills and reverberated through the maze of hills and flat-tops. The usual sounds of warfare, screams of the men, whinnying of the horses, rattle of sabers, and the blast of the bugle filled the valleys with the horror of the battle. Within moments, the sounds died down and the silence of the pines muffled the cries of the wounded.

Tate had seen the handful of men that escaped through the thick timber, but they were too far away for him to stop with his Spencer. He reloaded his rifle, climbed back aboard, and rode down the hill to rejoin the troops. As he rode through the trees, he saw the attack had been successful and the bodies of many Apache were scattered about. One soldier was being tended to as he sat against a tree, but no others showed wounds. When Tate approached Carson, the colonel said, "That worked quite well, don'tcha think? Twelve dead Apache and only one man wounded. But I guess some got away, but we'll get 'em. We'll get 'em!"

"From what I can tell, Mangas wasn't one of the twelve!" declared Tate.

"No, no he wasn't," answered Carson. "He's a slippery snake, ain't he?"

"I'm thinkin' he was headin' for that rancheria I spotted yesterday. If he gets them to join him, we'll have more trouble than we can handle," answered Tate.

"Then maybe we'll have to give 'em a little surprise," remarked the colonel, with a bit of a smirk on his face. He stepped down and put his hand on Tate's shoulder and started to walk into the trees beside his friend. He spoke to Tate about his plan, starting with, "Can you give Kaniache directions on how to find the trail to that village?"

"Yeah, believe I can. Once on the trail, it's easy 'nough to find."

"Good, then here's what we'll do . . ." and he laid out his plan for the village.

Two of the eight wagons that the troop started with had carried the barrels and carriages of twelve pounder mountain howitzers. By stripping one of the wagons of the wheels, the assembled howitzers were now trailing behind teams and led by Tate to the trail to the rancheria. The column had chosen to move cross country and through the maze of hills and mesas and timber to intersect the trail to the village and would meet up with the howitzers before approaching. Mid-afternoon saw the team leaning into their harness as they negotiated the trail, struggling at times on the narrow pathway. But when the column appeared, Carson dismounted, allowing the men to take a breather, before they prepared the attack.

Tate hadn't agreed with Carson's decision to use the howitzers on the village, but he also knew that if Mangas recruited more warriors, the balance of the battle would be turned in favor of the Mescalero. His responsibility was to again coordinate the attack by firing the first shot. Due to the vigilance of the villagers, the troops had to assemble further away, but still within sight of Tate, now seated on a high ridge above the village holding basin. When he saw the forces in position, he fired the big Spencer without taking aim at anyone in the village.

Suddenly, the howitzers blasted and the whistle of the projectiles over the treetops was the death knell for several. The explosion rattled the village and shocked all the residents. The shell hit on the far edge and exploded, destroying several wickiups and sending debris and bodies flying. Screams of women and children ratcheted through the rancheria as men scrambled for weapons, shouting for others to take cover. Another howitzer's boom sounded even as the first projectile exploded and the shell hit several yards from the first. The confusion of the people was apparent as women grabbed at children and men tried to protect their families with their own bodies. Two more thundering roars from the howitzers added to the cacophony and terror, each explosion destroying lodges and lives.

Four rounds were all that was ordered, and the troops had made their way to the village and now surrounded the encampment. When the villagers looked, they were frightened and sought to escape or at least to hide when they saw the blue-clad troopers sitting their horses, rifle butts on legs, and white men staring at the melee. The colonel fired his pistol in the air, and shouted, first in English then in Spanish, "Do not move! You are surrounded!"

Everyone stopped in place, looking from one to another, and one man, apparently a chief with hands uplifted shoulder high, began to walk toward Carson. As he neared, he spoke to the colonel, "I am Gian-na-tah, also called Cadete. This is my village. Why do you attack us?"

"I am Colonel Carson. My orders are to take the women and children captive and to kill all the men."

Cadete's eyes flared but Kit continued, "But I do not want to do that. Your people are to be taken to Bosque Redondo to the reservation. There you will stay, not to fight the white men anymore."

"I know of this place. It is a good place, but it is not our home. This," and he waved his arms around to indicate their village and the mountains, "is our home. We would stay here."

"If you do not go with us now, we will kill all the men and take the women and children captive," repeated the colonel, looking at those of the village.

The chief looked around at the many men in blue, then to the damage done by the howitzers, and looked back to Carson. "We will go."

CHAPTER SIXTEEN
APPEAL

IT WAS A SAD SIGHT TO WATCH AS THE TROOPERS PUT THE TORCH TO the many wickiups. The villagers were allowed to take an armful of possessions, mostly blankets and maybe a parfleche of foodstuffs, but all the weapons were confiscated, and the people moved away, heads hanging, as they followed the orders of Colonel Carson. The escorted captives and troop made it to the lowlands of the foothills where the scattered juniper and piñon provided little shelter as dusk dimmed the light and the cool of the evening chased away the hot afternoon's warmth. The Mescalero made their camp while Sergeant McIntosh stationed groups of men around the campsite to provide a continuous guard yet allow the men to make their camp and cookfires.

Tate had a restless night and rose early before the first light of dawn showed in the east. He went with Lobo to a bald shoulder of the last knoll of the foothills and found himself a seat on a broad moss-covered boulder to spend his time with his Lord. As was his custom, he started with the Scriptures, but the dim light made reading difficult and he set the Bible aside, put his elbows on his knees and began to unburden his heart to his God. "Lord, I'm troubled by the massacre of yesterday. Seeing those howitzer shells destroy the lodges and mangle those families, that couldn't be what you wanted. But, every time I think of that, the image of those mutilated miners comes as well. It's different when I'm fightin' for muh own life or those of my friends, but this, this war stuff, I just can't abide it. But I don't know what to do! Kit's my friend and I'm here cuz he said he needs me, but . . ." he shook his head as the confusing thoughts troubled him. He hung his head toward his folded hands, searching his memory for some thought, some scripture, anything that would give him direction or peace. The gentle breeze that often accompanies the coming light of dawn whispered through the nearby trees and Tate heard the flutter of pages from his open Bible. He looked down, then lifted the book and began to read the verse at the top of the page, he started at *Isaiah 55:8-9 For my thoughts are not your thoughts, neither are your ways my ways, saith the Lord. For as the heavens are higher than the earth, so are my ways higher than your ways, and my thoughts than your thoughts.* Tate lifted his eyes heavenward, "Now that ain't much help, Lord. I know that . . ." then lowering his eyes to the pages, "but I guess what you're tellin' me is to just trust you. Alright, I'll do my best, but these people are your people too, so, maybe you can send me a missionary, or someone, anyone to help 'em."

As the rising sun sent its brilliant shafts of gold to cross the sky, Tate felt the warmth on his face, and he rose to return to camp. Colonel Carson and his scouts met at the cookfire for their morning coffee and were enjoying the hot brew when the leader of the Apache, together with two others, approached. Cadete spoke, "We would talk with leader of the blue coats." He stood with arms folded across his chest, the other two men slightly behind him.

Carson stood as they neared and now answered, "I will speak with you. Sit. Would you care for some coffee?" he asked, motioning to the pot and cups lying nearby.

The chief nodded as all three men were seated on the grey log by the fire. Carson nodded to the cook, who poured the cups and handed them to the Mescalero leaders. Cadete began, "I am Gian-na-tah, known to the whites as Cadete. I am the leader of this band of my people. This man is Chato and this is Estrella. They are war leaders."

Both men nodded slightly at their introductions and Cadete continued, "We believe you attacked our village because of Mangas
Coloradas." He watched Carson's reaction, noticing the man nod in
agreement, "but he came to our village to get more warriors, but we
sent him away. We did not want our warriors to follow him."

"That is good. He will soon be taken if not killed. That was a good
decision on your part," answered Carson.

"We ask that you let us return to our village. There is much we
must do to prepare for winter, and you have destroyed our lodges."

Carson took another sip of his coffee, looked at Cadete, and
answered, "We cannot allow that. General Carleton has prepared a
place for you and your people at Bosque Redondo, and my orders are
to take you and your people there. The general has promised your
people will be cared for and food will be provided, as long as you
remain in peace at the reservation."

The chief leaned over and spoke with the others and for a moment
they had a strained discussion, then the chief turned back to Carson,
"We would like to speak with this General or someone that can order
us back to our home. Does this man have someone that gives him
orders?"

Carson grinned and shook his head, "Chief, everyone that wears
this uniform has someone higher up that gives orders. But that
general and others are in Santa Fe, and I am to take you to Fort
Stanton and later to Bosque Redondo."

"Could we go to Santa Fe to speak to these Generals?" asked the
chief.

Tate looked to Carson, "What would it hurt to let 'em have their
say? Them generals don't listen to us, maybe they'll listen to these
fellas?"

Carson looked from Tate to the leaders, "Tell ya what I'll do,
Chief. I'll let you and these two leaders go to Santa Fe to try to talk
some sense into these men, but I will still take the rest of your village
on to Fort Stanton. If you get those men to change their mind, then

we'll let your people return to your village, but if they don't, you'll have to come to Fort Stanton to be with your people."

"Then we will go to Santa Fe!" answered the chief, rising to his feet.

"Uh, yeah, but I'm sending some men with you," explained Carson, watching as the three men conferred again.

"It is a good thing. Maybe they will keep us from being killed like Manuelito and his men were killed," answered the chief.

As the three leaders started toward their people, Tate asked, "What did he mean about that Manuelito?"

Carson sat back down, looked to Tate, and explained, "Before all this stuff with the Confederates started, one of the Mescalero leaders, Manuelito, and several of his men were going to Santa Fe to try to work out a peace treaty. But one of those eager officers in blue attacked 'em and killed him and about a dozen of his men. That just made this whole Apache war that much worse. But that wasn't the only thing, there were others on both sides that just kept makin' things worse. All because none of 'em wanted to sit down and talk. Maybe these fellas goin' to Santa Fe will help, but I doubt it."

Carson sent for Sergeant McIntosh, and when he arrived, he instructed, "You pick out three volunteers, get supplies and ammunition for at least a week, then you will escort Cadete and his two friends, Chato and Estrella, to Santa Fe to see the generals. Maybe that Indian Agent, what's his name, Labadie, will be there too. These men want to talk 'em outta sendin' his people to Bosque Redondo. Either way, you're to bring them back. We'll be at Fort Stanton and if his folks can go home, so be it. But if not, then we'll have to take 'em to Bosque Redondo, if it's ready for this many."

"Yessir, will do sir. And sir, if they try to escape, what should we do?" asked the sergeant.

"Whatever you have to, so, you and your men stay alert. You'll be about two to three days gettin' there, and more gettin' back to Stanton."

"Understood, sir." The sergeant saluted and left to ready himself and his chosen volunteers.

BY NOON on the first full day of travel, they came upon the ruins of Tiwa Pueblo, an ancient pueblo built by the Tiwa people that fell to the Apache centuries earlier. At one time, it was rumored that this was also a mission of the early Spanish settlers, but now all that remained were crumbling adobe walls that kept the secrets of the ancients. Carson ordered the column to take their nooning in the shade of the few juniper or by the lows walls of the ruins. Tate and Kaniache were in the nearby hills and flats on their scout for the troops, hoping to prevent an unexpected attack.

The nooning was short-lived and Carson soon had the column back on the trail, bound to the south and eventually Fort Stanton. By dusk, they came in sight of the Quarai Ruins and chose to make their night's camp nearby. Cooky had finished his work just as Tate and Kaniache rode up to join the colonel for the meal, and with the usual greetings, they stepped down, stripped their mounts, rubbed them down and staked them on the patch of grass that flourished in the shade of the walls of the mission church. Tate looked at the ruins as he walked back to the fire and greeted Carson with, "That's quite the place, did you see how thick some o' those walls are?"

Carson chuckled, "Yup, I done checked it out. I heard about this place, there used to be a couple ranches here too, but the Apache burnt them out a long time ago, just like they did the mission. That mission dates back to the late 1600's, like that pueblo yonder." He nodded his head toward the camp of the others, near the ruins of what had at one time been a massive pueblo, but now was barely recognizable as anything but adobe ruins.

"This country sure has a lot of history," proclaimed Tate as he took a seat near the fire. Kaniache joined him and the cook served up plates of venison stew with biscuits. All the men eagerly consumed the food, saying little, choosing to tend to the more important matters of eating and drinking their coffee.

"So, see anything interestin'?" asked Carson.

Tate looked to Kaniache and the Indian nodded for him to speak. Tate looked to Kit, "Yeah, I think we found Mangas."

"You sure?" asked Carson, somewhat surprised at the report.

"He's a big 'un, alright. Compared to the usual Mescalero, he's head an' shoulders taller. If'n I didn't know better, I'd say his daddy was an Osage."

"Osage?" questioned Kit. "Don't think I know much about them."

"They're a tribe down Southern Missouri an' what they used to call Indian Territory way. I had some friends among 'em when I was younger. The men get to be, oh, a good head taller'n I am, sometimes more. Biggest one I ever did see was close to seven-foot-tall!" explained Tate.

"Hummph," grunted Kit, somewhat skeptical, "but what about Mangas?"

"There's a basin back toward that ridge of mountains yonder," he pointed to the west of their camp, "and I reckon 'bout an hour's, mebbe a little more, ride would take us there. From the looks of things, they've got 'em a semi-permanent camp there. Didn't see no women or kids, an' the lodges ain't permanent, just branches an' such. But I'd say they was campin' a while there."

"How many?" asked Kit.

Tate looked to Kaniache, and the Ute responded, "Two, maybe three hands. No more."

"Look like we could take 'em easy?" quizzed Carson.

"Not with the whole troop, but take a couple squads, no more'n a platoon, mebbe," answered Tate.

"This might be our last chance. We've got to turn to the east away from the mountains and move across the flats after this. I don't think he'd come after us, with no more'n he's got, but we might be able to get him. But, don't know 'bout leavin' all these," motioning to the captive Mescalero that numbered near two hundred, "with only fifty or sixty soldiers to guard 'em."

"Without their chief an' war leaders to stir 'em up, I think they'd be alright," mused Tate.

Carson looked at him, thought a moment, "Maybe you're right."

"Long as our people know what's goin' on, an' they don't. We might get out early and get back 'fore anybody gets any ideas," suggested Tate.

THE TROOPS WERE STRIPPED of anything that would make noise: canteens, sabers, loose scabbards, anything that could warn the Apache of their approach. Tate and Kaniache had the task of taking out any lookouts, all by the light of a waning moon and in the black timber. But the seasoned mountain man and native were up to the task as they crawled toward the camp, Lobo crawling beside them. The hours just before first light were the most difficult to stay alert, and the Apache were no exception. The first man, sitting against the tall spruce, nodded his head often, but did nothing to keep sleep at bay. With hand signals, Kaniache moved away, circling around the camp in search of another lookout. Tate gave him several minutes before starting his approach to his lookout.

With a signal to stay Lobo, Tate began bellying towards the man. The only light that filtered through the widespread spruce boughs came from the over-arching milky way, but it was just enough. The shadows parted as Tate neared, careful to avoid the whispers of buckskin against pine needles as he rose to his feet directly behind the big spruce. The pungent smell of sap did little to hide the scent of bear-grease in the hair of the Apache. Tate held the Bowie knife in his right hand, readying himself to take out the guard. The size of the spruce prevented him reaching around the trunk, and he set his feet to lunge forward. He thought of the muti-lated miners, and with a slow deep breath, he made one quick step, put his hand over the mouth of the guard and plunged the big blade into the startled man's side, just below the ribs, thrusting upward and twisting the knife as he skewered the man. Big eyes showed white as he tried to scream, pushing at his attacker, but knew he was dead where he stood. Slowly, he slumped, and Tate lowered the body to the ground.

Tate stood to look all around, searching the camp for any sign of arousal, but there was none. He was confident that Kaniache would succeed in taking out the other lookout, but they were not entirely certain there were no other guards. Tate motioned Lobo to go before him, and they circled the camp. When they came to Kaniache, the Ute using sign language, told Tate to go to Carson and give the go-ahead, while he made the rest of the circuit around the camp to eliminate any other scouts. With a nod, Tate turned back on his steps and with Lobo at his side, started toward the waiting Carson.

The colonel had elected to take only two squads of men, making a total of twenty-eight, counting the two scouts and the colonel. He was certain with the element of surprise enhanced with the smaller number, they would be able to subdue the Apache. Tate walked silently up to the waiting man, explaining the lay of the camp, and that Kaniache was ensuring there were no other guards.

"Good, good." Kit looked to a nearby man, "Sergeant Gibbons, you'll take First Squad and move along the slope on your left. Tate, you show these others of Second Squad where they need to be, and when you're in position, you start the ball! Remember, these are the ones that murdered those miners!"

Within moments, the men were positioned, and Tate fired the first shot. Immediately the other troops opened up with a volley that startled every living creature in the black forest. But the most surprising thing was the woods also erupted with gunfire. Seemingly from behind every tree came the blast of rifle fire, and in the camp, nothing moved. Tate shouted, "Take cover! Take cover!" The attack had been timed to begin at the first crack of dawn, and now that light made targets of all the men in blue. The Apache had been expecting them and turned the attack into an ambush.

To add to the insult, a large talus slope that jutted into the camp held a broad flat about twenty feet above the camp, and the notorious Mangas stepped out, shouted, "White man! You will all die! This is what we think of you!" He turned around and dropped his breechcloth showing his bare rump and bent over to slap it in derision toward the soldiers.

He was about two hundred yards away, and thought he was out of range of the soldiers rifles, but Tate dropped to one knee, brought up his Spencer and took careful aim, squeezed off the shot just as Mangas started to turn around. What Tate had aimed for was the back or side of the man, but the .56 caliber slug cut a furrow across both cheeks of the War Leader's rear. Mangas jumped as he pulled up his breech-cloth, danced around smacking at his own backside as if someone was standing behind him spanking, but even at the distance where Tate knelt, he saw blood painting the man's breechcloth, and he laughed as he pointed to the men, "Look at him dance!"

The reaction of the Apache to their leader's taunts, made them unconsciously expose themselves, and the troopers took advantage. Another volley erupted, and the pines did little to muffle the roar of the rifles as the blast reverberated through the mountainous terrain. Mangas had disappeared from his pulpit, and the constant gunfire subsided into scattered shots. When all fell silent, the men carefully began approaching the downed Mescalero and an occasional pistol shot sounded as some wounded man was dispatched.

Carson had been just behind Tate's line and was now beside the man as they picked their way through the trees. He saw Sergeant Gibbons and ordered, "I want a thorough search and when you find that Mangas, let me know!" With only a nod for response, the sergeant disappeared in the trees to carry out his orders.

Shortly, Kaniache came to their side and looked to Carson, "He and two others got away." He looked to Tate, grinning, "But he couldn't sit down!"

CHAPTER SEVENTEEN
SOLO

WITH FOUR DEAD AND THREE WOUNDED, THIS WAS THE COSTLIEST fight for the New Mexico Volunteers under Carson. But when the squads returned to the camp, they were met with the good news of the arrival of Major Hostettler and the rest of the command from Fort Marcy. The officers and scouts met around the cookfire and partook of some hot coffee. Carson looked to the major, "It's mighty good to see you, Major, I trust you had an uneventful trip with your captives?"

"Yessir, it was just that, uneventful. And we are ready to get back in the fight!" declared the eager officer.

"Well, now that the troop was back up to strength, we should have another uneventful journey to Fort Stanton," drawled the colonel.

"Stanton? I don't understand, sir," replied the major.

"We've been ordered to Fort Stanton, and we're to hold the prisoners there until sent for. Didn't you see Carleton at Fort Sumner?"

"No, sir. He was off to Santa Fe, and the Fort isn't complete, nor is the reservation ready for this many captives."

"And why not?" asked Carson.

"The usual, money. But they did get word before we left that another load of supplies was on its way, both for the fort and the captives. And, it looks like they'll be getting more troops, some of those boys from California."

Tate sipped at his coffee, listening to the interplay among the officers, their concerns about 'getting into the fight' and wanting to get 'blood on their sabers.' He looked at the different men, that under other circumstances would be talking about family, home, business, and their futures, but now spoke of death in the same manner as if discussing a card game. Tate had been struggling with the many battles, not just those here with the Apache, but the news that had been brought regarding the war in the east. Men killing men, many not understanding the why of it, but being used as pawns on a chessboard and knocked out of the 'game' just as easily. He stood, stretched, tossed the dregs of his coffee aside, and putting the cup down, walked away from the firelight.

He went to the edge of the trees, lifted his eyes to the starlit sky, and breathed deep of the desert air. There was the smell of dust, but also of sage, blossoming cacti, and rabbitbrush. The blend was made perfect by the cool of the night and the musk of sweaty horses and the wolf at his feet. It was quiet, save for the rattle of cicadas, and the distant wavering cry of a lonesome coyote that went unanswered. He pulled up a sandstone rock and plopped down, resting his elbows on his knees, then lifted his gaze to the dark silhouette of the flatland that was anything but flat.

He was lonesome for the soft touch of his woman, the laughter of his children, and the whisper of mountain air through the pines. His purpose of coming west so many years ago was to fulfill his and his father's dream of living in the mountains and enjoying the free life away from civilization, not to fight wars with Indians and shed the blood of others. He felt perplexed, troubled through and through. He learned loyalty at his father's knee, and that loyalty required him to help his friend, Carson. He didn't hate anyone enough to just kill them and had always measured his response in any conflict with the life and death of himself, his family, and his friends. Then and only then was he willing to shed the blood of another, but to sit and watch the cannon destroy the homes and lives of women and children, that was not the same. But if they hadn't done it that way, there would probably have been many more deaths, both among the Apache and the soldiers. He dropped his head again, shaking it side to side, pondering.

When the grey line in the east began to show color, Tate was saddling Shady and turned to see Carson coming toward him from the fire. "Goin' somewhere special?" asked Kit.

"Well, Kit, I need some time away from all this . . . whatever you wanna call it, so I think I'll just scout a bit further ahead than I have been. Me'n Lobo there, we'll leave markers for ya if'n we see anythin' that needs attention."

"Gonna be gone long?"

"Dunno. Didn't you say that Fort Stanton is four, five days straight south o' here on the east side o' them southern hills?"

"Ummhummm, 'bout that."

"Then if we don't see ya 'fore then, we'll see ya' there," answered Tate, pulling the girth tight. He chuckled and turned to face his friend. "You've got Kaniache and Big Nose, they'll keep you outta trouble. If that's possible, the way trouble finds you."

Carson grinned and chuckled, "Well, that's what happens when you put on this uniform."

"That's why you'll never find me in one o' them monkey suits," declared Tate. "And there's somethin' more."

"I thought so, what is it?'

"After we get to Stanton, I think I'm gonna head back to the mountains," said Tate, looking at his friend.

"Figgered as much. But, I've been mighty glad to have you with me on this trip. Not too many men I can count on like you."

The two men shook hands and Tate mounted up, looking down at the tousled hair of his friend sticking out from under the campaign hat. He picked up the reins as Carson said, "Straight south is the ruins of an old Spanish Mission called Quivira, good place to spend the night. Good cover."

"Gotcha," answered Tate, reining the grulla around to start into the sage-covered flat, the rising sun warming his left shoulder. He nodded his head, gigged Shady to a canter and was soon gone in a thin cloud of dust. Carson watched his friend ride and turned back for some more coffee before getting the troop on the move.

TATE BORE a little east of south with a distant landmark that of a long black gash of timber that split the browns and greys of the rolling flat-lands. The sun rose hot on his shoulders and sent rivulets of sweat coursing from his temples to his neck and chest. He had stripped off his buckskin top in favor of a cotton bib-front shirt he had traded for in Santa Fe, but it now hung limp with sweat. He began searching for a bluff or rock overhang that would provide him and his animals enough shade for a midday break and some relief from the merciless sun, and seeing a cut back in an arroyo, he dropped over the edge of the sandy bank to find just what he wanted. It was an undercut bank with a shelf of sandstone overhanging and giving shade enough for Lobo, Tate, and Shady.

With Shady on a long enough lead to reach a patch of grass, Tate lay back in the shade beside Lobo for a brief respite and a bit of a snooze. It was Shady tugging on the lead that woke him, and he slowly rose up to search his surroundings and was surprised to see a Mexican boy sitting beside Shady, stroking his head and talking to the horse. Tate frowned, looking around for others but seeing no one, he spoke softly, "Who are you?"

The boy, looking to be about nine or ten, didn't move but kept stroking the mane of Shady and looked to Tate, "I am Candelario Rodriguez, who are you?" he asked in broken English.

"I'm Tate. You live around here?"

"Si señor, not far," he answered, pointing to the southeast.

"Your family have a ranch?"

"Si. Not a very beeg one, but it is ours," answered the boy, obviously parroting his father.

"Are you hungry?"

"My Mamá says I am always hungry," came the reply from a wide smiling face.

Tate reached into his saddlebags and withdrew a packet of jerky and extended some to the boy. As he came near, Tate drew up his knees and leaned forward, "What are you doing out here away from home and all by yourself?"

The boy tore off a piece of the jerky with his teeth, then pointed down the arroyo to a small herd of goats grazing on the narrow strip of grass in the bottom. He mumbled through the mouth full of meat, "Cabras." He sat down in the shade, and leaning around Tate to look at Lobo, "That is a big dog, what is he called?"

"Lobo. But he's not a dog, he's a wolf."

The boy drew back and looked up at Tate, "A wolf? Why do you have a wolf?"

"He is my friend, and he's been with me a long time, since he was a little pup." Tate motioned Lobo to go to the boy, who hesitantly reached out to touch the big beast that dwarfed him. But they soon made friends, and the boy looked up at Tate, grinning.

"I have never seen a wolf. Mi padre say wolves eat cabras."

"Yes, and many other things as well. But he won't eat your goats."

The boy stood, looked at Tate, "Gracias for the jerky. I must go now, it will be near dark when I get home and mi Mamá, she worries."

"What about the Apache? Aren't you afraid of them taking your goats?" asked Tate, standing and pulling on Shady's lead to bring him near.

"I do not let them see me, but they don't like cabras. They want cattle or sheep or caballos. But the cabras need grass and we have none by our home, so . . ." and he shrugged his shoulders.

"What about your padre? Why doesn't he take the goats to grass?"

"Mi padre has been sick and there is no one else."

Tate watched as the boy started for the goats, "You be careful, Candelario!"

The boy turned, smiling, "Candy! Call me Candy. If you go south to the long ridge, our casa is near the big arroyo. You are welcome anytime, Señor Tate!" He waved and went to his goats, clucking and talking to them as he waved his staff to get them moving. Tate grinned at the boy, admiring his pluck and friendliness. He saddled up, rigged his gear, and stepped aboard the grulla, thinking all the while. Remembering his brief conversation with Candy and that his pa was sick, he thought the family was probably in need of some fresh meat. As he thought of some fresh venison steak, his mouth watered and he grinned, thinking he might just be able to help.

From atop a slight knoll, Tate used his scope to scan the jagged bluff that rose like a barrier across the flats. Covered with timber, the black of the forest contrasted with the browns of the flat land that cradled its cacti and sage. He searched for the brighter green that would mark fresh water, maybe a small spring fed pond or stream that would draw wild game. He slowly moved his scope, seeing no sign of life, until a small patch of green showed at a notch in the long rim-rocked ridge. He smiled as he slipped the scope back into the saddle-bags and gigged Shady forward. He stayed vigilant, for any Mescalero would know of the place for water and could already be camped nearby. He waved Lobo ahead to scout it out and followed at a quick trot, anxious to find a nice fat doe, or even an antelope, or desert bighorn.

He followed a finger of juniper and piñon that marked a runoff from the spring, staying under cover of the trees until he came to the thicker timber. Slipping his bow from the sheath and lifting the quiver from the tie by the cantle, he swung down, and loosely tethered Shady within reach of some bunch grass. He stepped through the bow to string the weapon, and nocking an arrow, he started his stealthy approach of the spring.

Three deer were bedded down back in the timber away from the water, and Tate readied his arrow, bringing the bow to full draw, and with a simple whistle, he brought the deer to their feet. He chose the nearest, a nice sized doe without a fawn, and let the arrow fly to its mark. The deer jumped when the arrow struck but was only able to take two steps before crumpling. The others quickly and quietly disappeared into the thicker timber as Tate waited for the quiet of the woods to return. He nocked another arrow and slowly walked to the carcass, checked to be certain it was dead, then with another search of the nearby area, he lowered the bow and began the field dressing of the animal.

IT WAS a simple and small adobe house with a window on either side of the door, a lean-to to one side and a rustic barn in the back. It sat back in the trees, giving room for a stick fence for the small corral for the goats, another lean-to for the milking platform and pegs on the wall for ropes and leads. As he approached, Tate saw a rifle barrel protruding from one of the windows, and he reined up, holding up one hand as he called out, "Is this the home of Candelario Rodriguez?"

The door was thrown open and Candy came out, grinning, "Señor Tate! Welcome!" He turned toward the house, "Mamá! He is my friend! Come see!" He turned back and went to his knees, calling Lobo toward him and the big wolf smiled and wagged his tail as he went to the familiar boy for some attention.

"Candy! That is a wolf!" proclaimed an excited woman as she saw her son petting the big animal. She held a hand to her mouth as she stepped back toward the door.

"It's alright, Ma'am, they're friends. He won't hurt him." Tate turned in his saddle and untied one of the hide bundles of meat, and looked to the woman, "I have some fresh venison here, I won't be able to eat it all before it spoils in this heat. Could you use it?"

Big eyes lifted to the stranger and she stepped forward timidly, "I am Rosa, Candy's Mamá, Gracias, señor," she answered as she reached up for the bundle. "Won't you stay and eat with us? My esposo, uh, husband, would like to meet you."

Tate looked down at the shy woman, "I'd like that. Si, I will stay."

He swung his leg over the cantle and stepped down. Looking to Candy, "Do you have some water for my horse?"

The boy jumped to his feet, "Si, señor. I will take him to water," and reached out for the reins.

"Whoa, wait a minute. Let me strip that saddle off and brush him a little first. Then he can drink."

CHAPTER EIGHTEEN
QUIVIRA

THE VENISON HAD BEEN CUT INTO THIN STRIPS, FRIED WITH WILD onions, some tomatillos, and peppers from the small garden, served up with some saucy rice. Tate grinned as he accepted another plate full, to the smiling appreciation of Rosa. "This is the best meal I've had since I left home!" declared Tate, grinning between bites showing his appreciation.

"We are very grateful for the meat, Señor Tate," replied Rosa, nodding toward her husband, Miguel. The man forced a grin and nodded in agreement.

"It has been hard since I have been so sick," interjected Miguel. He smiled to his wife, "But, I am getting better. My Rosa has been a wonder." He reached for her and they clasped hands, squeezing each other's and smiling at one another.

"I know what you mean, I've been missin' my wife somethin' terrible. I'm anxious to get back home," answered Tate, using a tortilla to clean his plate.

"When will you go home?" asked Rosa.

"Well, like I told you, I'm scoutin' for Colonel Carson, but I've told him after we get settled in Stanton, I'm headin' home. By the way," started Tate, looking to Miguel, "what can you tell me about that old Spanish Mission near here, Quivira?"

Tate noticed a strange reaction from Miguel as he asked, "Why do you ask?"

"Oh, just interested in history, I guess. My pa kinda got me into the study of it when he was still alive. He was a teacher and couldn't help himself, but most of his study was into the history of Saxons and the Britons and others of that era. But I've seen so much here in New Mexico, with the Tiwa Pueblos and Spaniards and others, it just kinda fascinates me. Carson said that General Carleton came through here and explored the Quivira some, so I thought I'd at least take a look-see."

Miguel visibly relaxed and began, "There have been some men that thought there was treasure there and have destroyed much. That is a place of the ancients. My ancestors, the people of the pueblos, told of the ancients living and trading with others at that place. They tell of men of metal hats and chests that came with one named Coronado who thought this was the place of gold. But there was none, yet that has not stopped others who believe there are treasures. The black robes of the Spaniards built many buildings of stone, places to worship and live. But the Apache and dry seasons drove them out and my people left. Now, it is nothing but stone walls that crumble." He dropped his eyes to the table, pushed his plate back, "And now, the Apache again try to drive everyone from these hills." He waved his arm around to indicate their homelands. He nodded to the southeast, "Those walls will still be standing long after we are gone and those after us as well. The spirits of the dead guard that place."

It was quiet for a few moments until Miguel pushed back from the table to stand. He looked to Tate, "Gracias amigo. You have given us meat and we are grateful. But I must return to my bed, I am tired."

Tate stood, shook the man's hand, "And I must be going as well. You," nodding to Rosa, "have been most gracious and I am thankful for the fine meal. But, I must be going."

Miguel looked at him again, "If you go to Quivira and mean to stay, do not stay in the churches. You will only be safe if you use the remains of a kiva or of the pueblo. The Apache sometimes use the churches, but the greatest danger at this time is the many rattlesnakes and scorpions," he held up his hands about eight inches apart, "this big and deadly."

Tate shivered a little; two things he did not like were snakes and bugs, especially those that were venomous. "I will happily avoid those places. But you say the remains of the pueblos are better?"

"Yes, I have never seen a snake in the pueblos."

"Good, then if I make it that far, I'll stay in the pueblos. Gracias amigo!" declared Tate as he stepped to the door. "If I'm ever back this way, I'll stop in!"

They nodded, shook hands and Tate went to the corral to fetch Shady. Within a short while, the trees obscured his view of the Rodriguez home and he looked to the sun, now on his right shoulder and lowering toward the hilltops. With better directions from Miguel, Tate rode up on the vast ruins just as the sun was painting the sky with shafts of gold and orange. Long shadows stretched from the walls, exaggerating the remains as Tate sat mesmerized by the scene before him. Grey granite walls, some standing ten feet tall, marked the largest sites, which according to Miguel's descriptions, were the churches. One obviously stood out with a wide entry holding a massive beam overhead and what must have been towers on either side, resembling the large cathedrals he saw in St. Louis. He shook his head in wonder as he rode among the remains, imagining the place busy with natives and black robes, even Spanish conquistadors. The entire ruins appeared to be a half mile long and a quarter mile wide. The largest buildings, probably the two churches, were built of quarried granite and limestone, and were about fifty by one hundred fifty feet, or larger.

He rode toward the larger remains of what had been a pueblo, easily recognized by the deteriorating walls of adobe brick. This had been a massive pueblo and he guessed this one alone housed three or four hundred people. He found a wall on the east side that stood over six feet and offered good protection, with trees and grass within a stone's throw. Tate chose that site for his camp.

The ruins were on the crest of a long, low knoll, but still the highest point for a great distance around. Tate chose to make his small fire under the wide branches of a large juniper, letting the dim smoke of the grey wood filter through the branches. The last thing he wanted to do was to broadcast his presence to any hostiles in the area; he wanted a good night's rest for a change. He made short work of fixing his pot of coffee and warming up the tortillas and strip steak packed for him by Rosa, and he sat back to enjoy his meal. He watched the sun slip below the low hills, making the uneven terrain a black line of demarcation, beyond which Tate was not prone to wander.

He had extinguished his fire, rolled out his blankets, and was close to turning in when Lobo growled, looking toward the granite ruins. Tate carefully peered over the wall at a notch to see a line of Mescalero warriors, followed by several burdened packhorses and other rider less horses, file into the walls of the largest church ruins. As he watched, the light behind the line made it difficult to make out the figures, but he was certain some of those on horses led by the warriors were women and children. He was troubled, unable to make out the figures with any certainty, but he somehow knew in his gut that they were not Apache women and children. Somehow, he would have to know for certain, it just was not in him to let things be, especially when he knew what the Apache had been known to do to captives. He breathed deep, lifting his shoulder as he shook his head, wishing he was anyplace but here.

He sat down, leaning his back against the wall with Lobo at his side, unconsciously running his fingers through the wolf's mane as he thought. Like a whisper in the night a scripture came to mind, Psalm 18:2-3. *The Lord is my rock, and my fortress, and my deliverer; my God, my strength, in whom I will trust; my buckler, and the horn of my salvation, and my high tower. I will call upon the Lord, who is worthy to be praised; so shall I be saved from mine enemies.* He had often read and re-read scripture, seeking to memorize different passages and as he looked at the walls around him, he knew it was for this time that he had locked that scripture in his heart. But he needed a plan to get to the captives and he didn't like where his mind was going. His father had always taught him to use what was available to get out of any predicament, but what was available, he didn't like.

He rose and went to his gear, bringing out a flour sack he had often used for carrying staples, but would now be used for other purposes. He saddled Shady, leaving a loose girth, but having him ready, just in case. He checked the loads on his pistol, then taking the longbow from its sheath, he strung the weapon and hung the quiver of arrows at his belt and started to leave, then as an afterthought, went into the trees in search of a long-forked stick. After a few moments, he had what he needed and by the light of the half-moon and the many stars, he quietly worked his way to the far church ruins, beyond where the Apache were bedded down.

As he stepped through the wide entry of the granite walled church, he stopped and searched, carefully scanning the stones and sandy floor of the structure. He was hunting, but not for Apache, but for another greatly disliked opponent, rattlesnakes. He knew the behavior of the reptiles, often using the sun-drenched stones to provide their needed warmth, but when the days were too hot, like they had been recently, the reptiles would come out after dusk and use the still warm stones to heat their bodies. He lay the bow aside, using both hands on the long-forked stick, ready to capture his prey. He knew he had to be careful, because rattlesnakes were ambush hunters, lying in wait for their prey and they were also known to hunt after dark. Tate measured each step carefully, searching the ground around for any indication of a snake. The sudden hiss and rattle startled him, and he froze, looking for the source. There on a wide stone, lay a big snake, head raised, tongue flicking, the tip of his tail twitching the rattles, and coils slowly moving back and forth. He was no more than six feet away, close enough for the scaly creature to strike, but Tate quickly lunged with the stick, catching it just behind the head and pinning it to the stone. As the body squirmed back and forth, Tate reached down, taking hold just behind the head, and dropped the stick to pull the sack from his belt. Holding it open, he lowered the snake, tail first, into the bag, quickly dropping the head in and clasping the bag shut, twisting it tightly to keep the snake from freeing itself. *That's one!* He thought, picking up the stick and carrying the bag at arm's length.

After he caught the second rattler, he had a dilemma. How to open the bag, insert a second snake, and not lose the first one. But he didn't have the time to consider, he just had to act, and he soon had the second and third snake in the bag. With all three snakes of considerable size, the bag was heavy and difficult to carry, but leaving the long stick and retrieving his bow, he carefully and quietly left through the entry. Using the shadows of the night, he moved to the far wall of the larger church where the Apache camped. The only lookout Tate had seen was a young warrior near the front entry of the ruins, and he had carefully avoided that part of the walls. He lay the bag down next to the wall and climbed up near the corner of the taller wall at the east end. He looked at each of the sleeping forms, determining the warriors, leaders, and captives by their position and nearness to others. The captives were bound and in the corner with warriors lying in such a way to be a barrier to the captives moving in any direction, should they be freed.

Further away, near their cookfire, several more warriors lay encircling the warm coals. As Tate searched, he counted a total of four captives, possibly three women and one youngster. And as near as he could tell, there were a dozen warriors. The horses were corralled in the end of the church, near the entry, guarded by the lone sentinel. Tate lowered himself from the wall, thinking and considering. Laying out his plan of attack in his mind, he started for the entry and the lone guard.

When he came to the corner, he slowly peered around, but the guard was nowhere to be seen. He waited, searching the area as best he could in the dim light of the moon, then thought the man must be just inside the entry, maybe using the walls to support himself as he stood in the dark. Giving Lobo the signal to stay, Tate slowly moved in the shadows of the wall, carefully picking each step, cautious of the many rock chips and pieces that could cause him to stumble. As he approached the entry, he heard the sound of heavy breathing and knew the guard was sleeping, but even a sleeping sentinel was dangerous. Without a whisper of a breath or touching anything that would be a give-away, Tate moved as slow and as cautious as a centipede, then saw the man, sitting and leaning against the wide entry wall. Tate quickly put a hand over the man's mouth as he drove the big-bladed Bowie into his chest, twisting the blade and practically disemboweling the man. The wide frightened eyes flared and a sudden push away from the wall, was the only movement left of the man as the light of life left his eyes and he went limp. Tate looked around, glad that the horses were inside a rope corral in the near corner, but the smell of blood made them a little restless. Tate pulled the body away from the entry and out of sight of the horses, laying it in the darkness at the base of the wall.

Stepping back into the entry, he went to the tethered end of the rope corral and cut it away from the partially rotted post, dropping it to the ground and moving away from the animals, letting them move of their own accord. But the horses didn't move, some standing hipshot and sleeping. Tate slipped away and returned to his previous spot near the far corner. He paused a moment, thinking, then returned to his camp and slung his Spencer over his back and returned to his point of attack. His chosen spot was at a crumbled corner, offering him a notch that would avail him of a shooting position for the bow. He made a circuit of the wall, making his plans, careful to not be heard, and returned to his first position.

Picking up the bag, he climbed the nearest spot to those by the fire. With most of the warriors there, he untwisted the bag, and with a single swing around, he sent the bag flying to land near the fire, knowing the snakes would quickly escape and with nowhere to go but away from the coals, they would have to crawl over and around the sleepers. As soon as he released the bag, he ran to the notch where his bow lay. He looked, seeing one of the sleepers rise, looking around, apparently wakened when the bag landed, but the bag was on the far side of the coals from the man and he lay back on his blankets. Tate had chosen his targets for the bow and now stepped into the weapon to send the first arrow into the chest of the man nearest the captives. With nothing more than a grunt at the impact, he was dead with the fletching stirring above his chest. The second arrow found its mark just as silently and the second guard of the captives was dead.

Suddenly, one of the men at the fire ring jumped and shouted, grabbing at his leg and screaming. He pointed as another big snake raised its head to strike at a rousing sleeper. The fangs were buried in the man's neck as he grabbed at the reptile and screamed. All the others had jumped to their feet, confused for an instant but seeing the snakes, some grabbed at rifles or pistols and started shooting. The rattle of gunfire split the silence of the night with explosions magnified by the near walls as the sounds bounced back and forth like the echoes in a deep canyon.

Tate had let one more arrow fly, burying itself in the chest of the first screamer, and the black arrow's fletching fluttered. The others saw the long arrow's point protruding out the man's back before he fell. Several frantically went to their gear, searching for powder and ball to reload their rifles, but the big Spencer boomed from the far wall and another man fell.

Tate jacked another round as he ran to his next chosen notch, cocking the hammer as he moved, then quickly using the stones as a rest, he took aim again and fired. Although it wasn't planned, the bullet tore through one man's side and another man, bending down to reload his rifle, caught the projectile in his head, killing him instantly. Tate, again on the move, found another break in the wall and sent a .56 caliber slug into the milling Apache, dropping just before a bullet from a Mescalero splattered against the granite brick beside him.

He moved back toward his first shooting position, wanting the warriors to believe there were many attackers, and using the top of the wall, he fired again, hitting a fleeing man in the lower back, causing him to plow dirt with his face. He saw the others trying to catch the now frightened horses, and he jacked another round, and fired into their midst, hoping to send them fleeing. He paused, watching them swing aboard the horses, lying low on their necks and making their escape. Four men were all he counted that made it to the horses, but some of the other animals fled with them.

Tate sat back, his breathing ragged, as he tried to let his mind catch up with his body, trying to think of all the warriors he had seen and where they might now be, maybe even searching for him. He went back to where he left the bow, picked it up and again climbed the rubble by the wall to look over where the warriors had been spotted. He searched the darkness for movement, and seeing none, he looked again, trying to locate the warriors that had been his targets. He reviewed his actions, looked to see the bodies, counted and searched again. Several minutes had passed and the remaining horses had settled down before he spoke. Looking at the shadows in the corner, he asked, "Are you able to talk?"

"You're American, oh, thank God!" came a voice from the darkness.

"How many are there?" asked Tate, speaking quietly and calmly.

"Three women and a boy," answered the speaker. "Are they gone?" she asked.

"Appears so, but I am going to check. I'll be back soon."

"Please hurry!" she pleaded.

CHAPTER NINETEEN
CAPTIVES

As Tate stepped into the large ruins, several horses cowered in the near corner and he walked to them slowly, holding out his hand and speaking softly. The first two sniffed at his hands, let him stroke their heads, and began to settle down. He looked at the five horses that remained, and tethered them together, tying off the lead to the same post that held them before. He slipped his Colt from the holster and walked to each of the downed warriors, ensuring they were dead by poking them with his foot and checking for other signs of life.

He picked his way among the bodies near the fire ring, one after another showed no sign of life, until one man groaned as he neared. Lobo growled, started toward one of the prone figures and was stopped by Tate's word. The man lay on his side, holding his leg, as Tate saw this was the first man bitten by the snake. When he saw Tate approach, he tried reaching for his rifle that lay nearby, but Tate kicked it away, holding his pistol on the man. "I don't know if you understand me, but," nodding toward the man's leg, "you're not gonna make it. That snakebite looks bad."

The man looked at Tate and Lobo, then around at the other dead men, reached for the knife at the belt of one then paused, looking back to Tate. "Go ahead," said Tate, nodding toward the knife. The man withdrew the knife, looked at his leg and took a deep breath, then cut across the fang marks, letting the blood flow down his leg. Tate watched as the man scooted back against a large stone, keeping his leg outstretched, massaging it to make the blood flow. Tate walked among the other bodies, but no others lived, noting the remains of the snakes that had been shot to pieces by the alarmed Apache, and chuckled. He picked up the weapons of the dead men and stacked them well away from the snake bit man, and stepped back near the him, still working his leg to keep the blood flowing. "I'm gonna get those women," nodding toward the corner of the ruins where the captives waited, "and if I see you move, I'll shoot." He had pointed and motioned with his pistol to emphasize his words. Then as a second thought, he holstered the pistol and used sign language to explain. The Apache nodded his head in understanding and looked back to his leg.

Then looking to Tate and using sign, he asked if there was any buffalo root nearby.

Tate thought a minute, nodded his head and signed, "I saw some by my camp. I will free the women, then bring you some."

The man dropped his eyes as Tate stepped back, keeping a watch on the warrior, motioning for Lobo to stay and watch the man, then made his way to the women. All were bound hand and foot and in the dark corner it was difficult to make them out, but as he approached, "Ladies, we need to get a move on and hightail it out of here. Now, I'm gonna cut you loose but don't go runnin' off cuz there's snakes about."

He heard the gasps of alarm from the women and let a bit of a grin split his face as he went to a knee and cut the bonds on the first woman's feet, then her hands. Once freed, she threw her arms around Tate's neck and sobbed, "Thank you, thank you, thank you!"

Then a voice came from the darkness, "Señor Tate? Is that you?"

Tate frowned and moved closer to the next woman, barely able to make out her features in the dim starlight, "Rosa?" he asked.

"Señor Tate! It is you!" came the familiar voice of Candy Rodriguez.

He quickly cut at the bonds of Rosa, and turned to the next

woman, as he spoke, "What about Miguel?" he asked, assuming the worst.

"Just after you left, he heard a noise outside and thought you might have returned, but as soon as he stepped out the door, the Apache," she spat the word, "shot him full of arrows! Then they took us before we could do anything. They killed all the goats and burnt everything!" She sobbed at the last, rubbing her wrists and ankles.

"Who is with you, Señor Tate?" asked Candy.

"Just me'n Lobo, Candy."

The third woman, finding her voice, "You did all this, by yourself?" she asked incredulously.

"No ma'am, I had the good Lord's help."

He stood and helped the ladies to their feet, then looking to Candy, "How 'bout you takin' the ladies to the horses yonder and pick out some you can ride. We'll be takin' outta here right quick."

"Si, señor," answered Candy, taking his mother's hand and starting toward the entryway and the horses.

Tate walked back to the snake bit warrior, who still watched him. "I'll get that root for you. I'll even make a poultice for you. If you live and get better, there'll be a horse back there," motioning toward the corner of the church. "He'll be tied loose in case he has to get away, but he'll be there long enough for you, if you make it."

Tate went to the notch in the wall, climbed over, watched Lobo take a couple of steps on the rocks then with one long leap, clear the top, and land quietly on the other side. Tate bent and fetched his bow and quiver, then went to Shady. He tightened the girth, slipped the bow in its sheath, hung the quiver, and taking the rifle from its sling on his back, he swung aboard and slid the Spencer in the scabbard. He had spotted some osha or buffalo root nearby, rode to the spot, and dropped down to pull it up. He wiped the dirt off the root, and quickly made a poultice with the mashed root by using the nearby stones. He remounted and went to the main entry where the women and Candy waited.

Each woman stood, holding the leads on their chosen horses, and

Tate said to Candy, "Tie that other'n loose in the corner there. Make sure it's loose enough that if he needs to pull free, he can." He looked at the others, "I'll be right back."

As he neared the Apache, the man, obviously in pain, breathed heavy and looked at Tate. Tate knelt down and put the big poultice on the open wound and patted it down. "That might help, but . . ." He looked at the man who was staring back at him.

"Why do you do this?" asked the man, in stilted English.

Tate, surprised at the man's talk, answered, "Why not? You're hurt, need help. I don't hate you. I just did what I had to cuz of the women and the boy."

"How are you called?" asked the man.

"Longbow. That's what most natives call me. Whites call me Tate Saint. How are you called?"

"Santana. Son of Barranquito. Brother of Cadete."

"Cadete's brother? He and his people are now with Colonel Carson."

The man's eyes grew large in alarm, "Cadete?"

Tate nodded, "Yup, he surrendered his village. Didn't want any more bloodshed. If you live," nodding toward his leg, "you might wanna think about that yourself."

Tate stood, looking down at Santana, "I left the horse like I said. But I'm takin' those rifles and ammo," pointing toward the stacked arms.

Santana nodded, and leaned back, resting his head on the stone, and watched Tate carry the three rifles and two pistols away. Tate intentionally left the bows and arrows behind for the warrior, he would need something to hunt with and no man should be alone in the mountains, unarmed.

TATE WANTED to be as far away from the Quivira ruins as possible. He knew the four Apache that fled would probably bring others back, if for nothing else than to retrieve their dead, although the Apache were not as concerned about their dead as he had known other native tribes were, but they still preferred to bury them. As was his custom, before dark settled, he had picked out landmarks for his route and now, with the darkness of early morning, the distant hills showed as looming shadows. With the women, now each one armed, and Candy in his charge, he preferred to travel at night and wanted to find a camp before full light of day. He estimated the hills to be about fifteen miles distant, but the preferred campsites would be within the trees at the foot of those hills.

They were traveling due east, but Tate chose to turn more to the south. Of the two low peaks that were his chosen landmarks, the more southerly and smaller one became his guide. Shortly after leaving Quivira, the juniper and piñon became more sparse and finally gave way to nothing but sage and buffalo grass and the ever-present cacti. Patches of prickly pear threatened as thorny beds had little to mark their presence in the dark. But the cholla appeared as dark skeletons lifting bony limbs as specters of the night. When a jackrabbit bolted from under some greasewood, Shady jerked his head back and side-stepped, waking Tate from his slumber in the saddle. He chuckled as he reached down to stroke the horse's neck and speak softly to him. "So, you were dozin' too, eh boy?" He twisted around in his saddle to look to the others, and all were slumped forward, one of the ladies even lay along the neck of her mount, fingers twisted in the mane to hold on in her torpor.

He turned around, stood in his stirrups to try to see a bit further, and with nothing but darkness and shadows, he sat back and looked to the horizon, guesstimating the time until sunrise. With the terrain becoming more difficult, the ladies were stirred by the aggravated movements of the horses, and Rosa asked, "How long before we stop?"

"Oh, 'bout an hour or so. I want us to have some better cover, hopefully in the trees. We'll rest most of the day before we start out again. It'll be safer travelin' at night." The women were too tired to respond, but neither did they complain.

They were facing into the rising sun before they came to the trees

at the foot of Tecolote Peak. Tate had let Shady have his head and he
followed an arroyo that bent back upon itself and opened into a basin
with tree covered slopes all around. Light green leaves marked water
at the head of the draw and Tate chose the well covered area for their
camp. Once stopped, the women slid from the horses and stretched
out on the ground, weary from their ride and the tribulations of the
day before. All were somber and disconsolate; Tate had only heard the
story of the attack on the Rodriguez home, not knowing who these
other women were or what happened. He didn't question them as he
stripped Shady and led him to the water. Candy led his horse to stand
beside Tate and stood silently, watching the animals slake their thirst.

When Tate returned, he spoke to the weary women, "Ladies, you
need to take care of your horses. Rub 'em down with some o' that
bunchgrass yonder and lead 'em o'er there to get some water. If you
don't take care of them, you'll be walkin' and I don't think you'll like
that."

The ladies sat up, looked at Tate, then to their horses, and each
one slowly rose and went to their animals. Tate was more concerned
about the women than the horses, but he thought it would be good for
them to be busy. He motioned for Candy to fetch some firewood and
Tate gathered the necessities together to fix some coffee and cook
some venison strips. They would be on sparse rations for a couple
days, but at least they wouldn't go hungry.

When the women finished with the horses, they returned to
where Tate had a small fire going and the coffee pot heating. He
finished cutting strips of venison and hung them on some green locust
limbs to broil over the fire. He sat back on a rock, waiting for the
coffee and looked at the women. Rosa sat nearby, but the other two
were beside one another, staring into the flames as they sat on a grey
log. Tate asked, "Ladies, I'm Tate, and this lady is Rosa Rodriguez and
that young man yonder is her son, Candelario, or Candy. They only
know me cuz I stopped by their house yesterday and had a bite to eat.
Now, you heard her tell me about what happened at their home, do
you feel up to telling about yourselves?"

The women looked at one another, and with a slight nod from the younger one, the older of the two, a woman of about forty, began, "I am Felicia Almanzar, my husband, David, and I had a ranch that was in our family for three generations and a part of an old Spanish land grant. She," nodding toward the younger woman, "is Louisa Fontenot. We are sisters. She and her husband partnered with us and invested in the cattle and the ranch. We have lived peacefully there in the midst of all the wars with the Apache and Navajo and the war with Mexico, but now the Apache suddenly attacked us, killing everyone. Our husbands, our children, and our other workers and their families, all dead," she sobbed, lifted her head and breathed deep to continue. "We were taken prisoner and forced to watch them torture our husbands until they died. When we left, everything was burning, and our children were in the house as it burned." Both women started weeping at the thought of their children dying in the flames.

Tate looked to Rosa, who stood and went to the women, touching their shoulders but saying nothing, just being there for them. Tate's shoulders heaved as he shook his head, marveling at the strength of the women but angered at the cruelty of the attackers.

"Well, ladies, we're going to Fort Stanton. You'll be safe there until you decide what you want to do. You'll have all the help you need for whatever you choose." He wanted to say more but knew now was not the time for what would be thought of as empty platitudes. Now, they needed time to grieve.

CHAPTER TWENTY
SOUTH

TATE AND LOBO SLIPPED AWAY FROM CAMP MID-AFTERNOON, BUT HAD not gone far before the voice of Candy beckoned, "Can I come with you?" Tate turned, grinning, and motioned for the boy to join him. The women had been restless early on, but now seemed to have settled down and were sleeping sound, and Tate planned to improve their larder, knowing they could use some meat for the next couple of days before they would reach Fort Stanton.

Candy looked at Tate's longbow and up at the man, "Why don't you have your rifle?"

"Makes too much noise. I'd just as soon nobody know we're here. 'Sides, I can take just about anything with this that I can with a rifle," he replied, nodding towards the bow.

"I never shot a bow before," answered Candy, looking at the long weapon.

"Well, it takes considerable practice 'fore a man is any good with one. Indians use 'em from the time they're wee little," motioning with his hand held about waist high. "And this'ns called a longbow, and it takes a lot to draw. Most can't, but I've used one since I was 'bout your age and have learned by long hours of tryin'."

All the while they talked, they walked, searching the trees for any game. They came to a talus slope, large boulders looking like the Creator had stacked atop one another and went to the top of the heap for a look see. Searching the tree-line along the slope and above and below them, Tate watched the boy, waiting to see if he would spot what he had seen. Suddenly, the excited boy pointed to the flats, "Antelope! Cinco!"

Tate grinned, "Yup, but they're a little too far for me to take with the bow. But, tell you what, let me show you an old trick."

He stood and turned back toward the trees, Candy and Lobo following. Working his way around the finger ridge and along the tree line, he paused and pulled his neckerchief off. "Now, I'm gonna put this on you, but leave the long end on your shoulder. There's just enough breeze to make this work. Now, here's what you're gonna do . . ." and he detailed to the boy where and what he was to do and watched as he climbed to the crest of a small empty knoll and sat down, knees drawn up and arms clasped around them. Tate grinned as he watched the boy do exactly as he had been told.

Tate carefully made his way through the scattered juniper and cedar, swinging wide of the boy's perch, but closer to the flats and the antelope. He found a perch behind a thin piñon and sat down to wait. Lifting his eyes to the sun, he guessed it to be late afternoon, probably nearing five. He watched the antelope as Lobo stretched out for a snooze. Within a few moments, Tate noticed one of the antelope staring at the boy but standing unmoving. The buck dropped his head, grazing on the gramma, appearing disinterested. But soon he lifted his head to look at the boy again. Tate looked at Candy, saw the scarf rippling in the breeze and Candy staying absolutely still. Again, the buck dropped his head, but not after taking four or five steps in the direction of the knoll.

This action was repeated several times, with each time bringing the speedster of the plains closer to the mound. Tate waited, watching, as the buck and others slowly drew nearer. Finally, when the buck was within about fifty yards of the knoll and forty yards from Tate, he slowly rose, staying behind the tree, and nocked an arrow. With barely perceptible movement, he pushed into the belly of the bow, bringing the arrow to full draw, and let the missile fly. Antelope are quicker and more skittish than deer or elk, and the buck turned his head at the whisper of the shaft, but before he could spring away, the arrow pierced his side, impaling itself in his chest. The shock of the penetration startled the buck and he sought to flee, but his usual leap of escape failed, and he fell to the ground. The other animals were gone in an instant, disappearing in tufts of dust.

Candy jumped to his feet, "You got him!" he shouted, and ran toward the downed tan and white carcass. Lobo had come to his feet at the first movement of Tate, and now looking at his man as if seeking permission to go, Tate nodded, and the wolf scampered to meet Candy at the downed buck. Lobo had always had an affinity for children and reveled in the attention from the boy as he rubbed the scruff of his neck and hugged him.

As Tate began the field dressing, he explained what he was doing to Candy who stood close beside him, watching every stroke of the big Bowie. "But I don't understand why I was on the hill with the scarf," asked the boy.

Tate chuckled and said, "A Ute Indian friend of mine showed me that trick. You see, Antelope have better eyesight than we do and can see the smallest details and movement from a long way off. But they're also mighty curious. So, when something unusual popped up, you, and then didn't move, they were curious. But when the scarf flopped in the wind, that got their attention and when it didn't look dangerous, they just had to see what it was and to do that, they had to get closer. Just like you and I do when we want to see something better. But, and here's a lesson for you to learn, that curiosity got him killed."

As they walked back into camp, an excited Candy ran to his mother, "Mamá, did you know that curiosity can kill you?"

The astonished Rosa looked at her son, questioningly, then looked to Tate. The man was chuckling as he dropped the hide bundle of fresh meat, and she looked back to her son. "Si, I know that, but how do you know that?" As Candy began to tell of his adventure with Tate, she sat down, motioning for him to sit with her, and patiently listened to all the details. She nodded her head as he spoke, occasionally glancing at Tate, but enjoying the attention and excitement of her son.

Tate noticed the women had taken some pains with their appearance. Before, their hair was tangled and mussed, dresses hung in tatters, and dirt was their only adornment. But now, they had washed themselves, attempted to repair their clothing and did their best at fixing their hair. Tate was pleased that they were showing concern for themselves, for he knew that grieving people seldom paid attention to their appearance or attire. This was a positive sign the women were at least looking ahead.

The sisters had assumed the task of slicing off some meat and fixing some coffee. Rosa had found some onions and prickly pear blossom fruit to add to the fare and the women were busy at their task. Tate walked to the stack of gear and began to examine the weapons. The three rifles were all cap and ball Hawkens, and the pistols were a .44 caliber Walker Colt and a .36 caliber Colt Paterson. Tate checked the loads in the pistols and, satisfied, checked the Hawkens. After a thorough examination of the possibles bags and powder horns, he walked back to the small fire. He grinned as he noted the women had shown the good judgment of using only the driest wood and used the fire ring that Tate used, keeping the fire under the wide branches of the juniper letting what little smoke there was be filtered through the branches.

"You ladies know much about firearms?" he asked of the group.

All three stopped what they were doing and looked at him like he was asking a very stupid question. "What?" he asked. "I need to know," he explained, waiting for an answer.

Louisa, the younger of the sisters, answered, "A woman doesn't grow to adulthood in this country without knowing how to shoot!" she explained, then turned back to the pot of stew. The other women dropped their eyes and busied themselves.

"Alright. That was a dumb question. But I think what I was wanting to know was if you were familiar with these particular weapons. You know, how to reload 'em and such."

"Yes," came the answer, almost in unison, from all three women.

Tate shrugged his shoulders, looked at Candy, "Help me out here Candy. We men need to stick together."

"Si, señor, but you should know, it was my mamá who taught me how to shoot."

Tate shook his head, looked to Lobo, "You still like me, don'tcha boy?" and the wolf looked at him, went to lick his face, then turned away and went to the boy and lay down beside him. The women had watched the interchange and when Lobo flopped down, they all laughed, and the laughter was catching and soon everyone was laughing together. It was a good relief for everyone.

Tate had used his tomahawk to fashion platters from split wood for each of the women, but they had to share the two cups for the coffee. As they ate, Tate explained, "We're about two days out of Fort Stanton. We'll be traveling after dark, little safer that way, and staying near the tree line. I know riding astraddle and on blankets ain't the most comfortable for you ladies, but it's the best we can do, but I do want you to let me know if we have to stop."

"What's to happen after we get to Fort Stanton?" asked Felicia.

"I reckon that'll be up to you. Do you have any other family?" asked Tate.

"We had a brother, but he was also killed. No other family."

"You still own the ranch, maybe after Carson gets these Mescalero on the reservation, things'll settle down and you could return there. Maybe try to put things back together, or . . ."

"Perhaps," replied Felicia

"What about you, Rosa?" asked Tate.

"I do not know. I have no family, no money, and now no home," she dropped her head but pulled Candy close.

Louisa spoke up, "Maybe you could come with us?" looking from her sister to Rosa.

Felicia smiled and said, "We will need lots of help, and it would be good for all of us to be together." Rosa smiled, nodding and dabbing at a tear that threatened to escape.

"Well, whatever you decide, I know Carson well enough that he'll do anything he can to help. I think he'll be takin' all the Mescalero north to Fort Sumner and Bosque Redondo, and maybe that'd be the time to get you ladies back north to your ranch. But whatever it takes to get you all settled, I'm sure he'll help out." He looked around, "But for now, we need to get packed up and ready to go. We won't hafta wait for full dark, and we can make time in the dusk."

THE DIM SHADOW of a tall peak was his chosen landmark as they started almost due south from their camp. Once clear of the sparse juniper and piñon, the terrain showed little challenge. With one low rise that blocked his view of the landmark peak, Tate relied on the North Star at his back to keep his direction. Before midnight, the peak was off his right shoulder and he searched the moonlit flats for another goal that would keep them on the south bound course. He split two lesser peaks, keeping to the lowlands between the hills and nearer the thicker trees, and pushed on. In the distance rose a dark peak, with another band of taller mountains beyond. Remembering the description of the trail by both Carson and Miguel Rodriguez, he recognized the more distant range as the last obstacle before reaching Fort Stanton, but that would be too far for this night's travel.

By the first hint of dawn, they neared a saddle between two taller hills, all covered by timber, and promising a possible camp. Once atop the saddle the grey light in the east showed a basin with greenery that enticed them to make camp and hopefully have ample water and graze for the animals. He gigged Shady forward to lead the way, just as anxious as the others for a time to stretch, eat, and get some rest. It had been a good night of travel, the best kind, no Apache. But tomorrow held no guarantees.

CHAPTER TWENTY-ONE
FLIGHT

TATE USED THE LATE AFTERNOON WHILE THE WOMEN STILL DOZED TO check the loads in all the rifles and pistols. Although he had done it before, he just wanted to reassure himself the weapons were usable and ready. As the women began to stir, he rekindled the small fire, pushing the refilled coffee pot nearer the flames and hanging the strips of meat over the fire. The women, one at a time, stood, stretched and made their walk into the bushes to quickly return.

"I thought we'd try to get an early start and hopefully make it the rest of the way to Stanton by mornin'," he drawled, speaking to no one in particular. He wiped his coffee cup dry, sat it on the rock and picked up the other one to do the same. "Soon as one o' you wanna watch the meat, I'll rig up the horses," he offered.

"I'll do it," answered Rosa, walking to the fire.

Tate nodded and went to the horses. He put on the headstalls, blankets, and girths, and turned to Shady to saddle and bridle him. He had offered to let one of the ladies use his saddle, but they declined, refusing to allow him to give up his seat. They also knew his weapons were rigged to the saddle and they knew he needed quick access. When the horses were ready and tethered to the trees, he returned to the fire and plucked a strip of meat, still sizzling, from a branch and made short work of the simple fare. With a quick chug at his coffee, he surrendered the cup for the use of the ladies and walked to the edge of the trees to survey their route. Candy followed and stood beside him and asked, "Where are we going this time?"

Tate grinned and looked down at his helper, then dropping to one knee beside the boy he started to point out their route, but paused, smelling the smoke from the fire, and realizing how easy they could be found just by that. He looked to Candy and began, "See that mountain yonder," pointing to the southeast, "and these lower ones closer up and over this'away?" He pointed to a continuous range of timber covered hills that raggedly reached for the sky but failed. He looked down to Candy who was nodding his head. "Well, we're going through that low spot there, keeping the bigger mountain off our left shoulder. Once through there, we'll keep goin' south and come onto Fort Stanton."

"How do we know which way is south?" asked the boy.

"Well, for right now, we use the sun." He turned to face the lowering fireball, "Ol Sol there always goes down in the west and comes up in the east. Now, in the afternoon, he's in the west, and if you face to the west, then south is to your left and north is to your right," at each direction, he turned to face that way, emphasizing his instruction. "Understand?"

"Si, si. But what about at night when we can't see the sun?"

"That's a good question, and once we're on the way, I'll show you. You see, there's a star called the north star that's always in the same place. And you can use it to know which way you're going."

"When it's dark, you'll show me?" asked the curious boy.

"Si, si. I'll show you," answered Tate, standing and putting his hand on Candy's shoulder.

As he turned, he saw the women waiting by the horses and he looked to Candy, "Looks like they're ready to go!"

"We better hurry," answered a laughing Candy.

Once clear of the trees, Candy rode beside Tate and quizzed him again, "Is it dark enough to see the north star?"

Tate looked to the west as the colors of the sunset faded, then stood in his stirrups to turn and look behind them. There were just a couple of stars in the sky, the few remaining long lances of color from the setting sun making it impossible to see the dimmer lights of the heavenly bodies. Tate looked to the boy, "Not yet. But you can watch the sky behind us, and you might see it before I do!"

Then something registered in Tate's mind and he turned back around, lowering his eyes to the flats behind them instead of the sky. There, the rising dust of running horses gave them away. He snatched at the saddlebags for his scope, swinging Shady crosswise of the trail and lifting the scope to his eye, one quick scan showed what he feared, Apache! And it looked like eight or ten of them. He quickly stuffed the scope back, reined Shady around and hollered at Candy. "Run! Lead 'em where I showed you!" Then turning to the women, "Candy'll lead you! Go! Apache!" he pointed behind them and reached over the slap the rear of Rosa's mount. The horse lunged forward as he hollered at the sisters, "Go! And keep going! Don't stop!"

He slapped the other mounts and swung around to follow. They were at a full all-out run, hooves kicking up dirt and rocks, riders laying low on the necks of their animals, and Tate saw at a glance these women knew how to ride! He knew their chances of outrunning the Apache were slim at best, but they had to get as far as they could. He searched the dim lit flats for any possible cover, planning to send the women on before he stopped to try to slow or stop the attackers.

He twisted around to see how close the attackers were, then back to the front, searching for cover. Suddenly, he saw the horses ahead drop into a wash and quickly mount the other side, hardly losing a step. He knew that was as good as he would find and as he neared, he slid Shady to a stop, dropped into the narrow wash and with one hand untying the saddlebags and the other on the Spencer, he soon hit the ground and bellied down on the near bank. He watched the Apache coming and lay the saddle bag at hand, checked his Spencer and grabbed a flat piece of sandstone to use for a rest and took aim. Bringing the Spencer to full cock, he followed the leader as he neared, but with the man lying low on his mount's neck, it would be a difficult shot, but he had no choice. He squeezed the trigger and without waiting to see if he scored a hit, he jacked another cartridge into the chamber, cocked the hammer, aimed, and fired again.

He suspected the Apache had expected him to have to stop and reload, as they kept up the charge, slowing after the second shot. He saw two men and one horse on the ground as he took aim again. Within less than a minute, he had fired the Spencer seven times, emptying the tube and now grabbed for a tube of cartridges. He had several of the Blakeslee tubes, each with seven cartridges, and he knew he might have to use them all. In seconds, he brought the rifle up for another round, but the Apache had taken cover. He searched the area before him, seeing only an occasional clump of sage or greasewood, and with the dim light of dusk, he knew the Apache knew where he was, but he didn't know where they were, and they could be anywhere in this light.

He breathed deep, took a quick glance to see Shady standing, ground tied, and head hanging as if he was dozing. Lobo was at his side, looking from his man to the dry terrain beyond. Suddenly the ground heaved forth and five warriors rose up and charged, screaming war cries. It was too easy for Tate, first one, then another and another fell from his rapid fire, and just as suddenly there was no one. Silence dropped like a blanket across the flats, nothing moved, no sound came until a slight moan from one of the men, apparently still alive though having wounds serious enough to keep him down.

Tate considered, trying to think of how many there were, but knew he hadn't been able to get a good count. He was too busy trying to get the women away, but as he considered, he had dropped at least three on the original horseback charge, three more when they came on foot. But he had estimated there were eight or ten. The odds were still against him. He rose up for another look, then cast a glance toward the west to see how much light might be left. Then out of the light came a warrior running at him, screaming. Tate swung the rifle around, cocking it as he moved, and fired the big gun without aiming.

Flame came from the attacker and a sudden blow to Tate's head knocked him backwards. He grabbed at the air, losing his grip on the Spencer and as he fell, he thought it had suddenly gotten awful dark. He didn't feel himself hit the ground, and all he saw was blackness and all he heard was silence, peaceful silence.

SOMETHING WET MOVED across his face, and he tried to open his eyes. As he tried to squint, another slobbery wetness brought him awake. The big red tongue of Lobo was a welcome alarm and he rubbed his face on the scruff of the wolf's neck before he realized where he was and what had happened. He quickly looked around; the darkness bathed the land, but the stars and moon shared enough light for him to see the shadowy still form in the bottom of the arroyo. One of the Apache was sprawled on his back and blackness covered his face, neck and chest. Tate knew that was blood. He looked at Lobo and saw blood on his jowls and said, "Thanks buddy. You done it again and saved my hide." He looked for his rifle, picked it up and checked the load, jacked another cartridge and cocked the hammer before searching the rest of the flats around them. As he replaced his floppy hat he watched, but nothing moved, and the bodies of the attacker still lay spread-eagled where they fell. He waited, watching, but there was nothing. With another deep breath, he heaved his shoulders and slipped down the bank to Shady. Mounting up, he held the rifle across the pommel and gigged the grulla out of the wash and started in the direction shown by the tracks of the women's horses.

He had gone but a short distance when he saw three sets of tracks coming from the side and following after the others. He looked again, closer, and saw two were unshod ponies, and one was shod. He guessed they were Apache, one with a stolen horse and probably had circumvented him and the wolf in favor of pursuing the women. He spoke to Shady and Lobo, "Alright boys, we need to get to them women 'fore those "Pache!" and kicked Shady into a ground-eating lope.

. . .

THEY MADE it to the low cut between the timber-covered mountains. Candy had kept up a hard pace and as they rounded the point of timber, his horse stumbled and he reined up, knowing the animals were about give out. He reached down to pet the horse's neck and he felt the lather of heavy sweat; the horse's sides heaved, and his head hung. Candy looked at the other mounts and looked to his mother, "Mamá, the horses!" he exclaimed, pointing to the animals.

"I know Candy. We have to stop." She turned around to look behind them and seeing nothing, she turned back to survey the area nearby. She spotted some green, "There!" she exclaimed as she pointed. They started for the trees, anxious for some reprieve and shelter. There was water, but very little. It was a small tank of runoff, stagnant, but wet enough. The horses drank, but their riders pulled them back after just a short moment, then led them to some grass just inside the trees. Candy looked at the women, watching them find seats on rocks and a log, and he stood before them. "Señoras! We must prepare for an attack by the Apache. If Señor Tate cannot stop them, we must fight!"

Rosa smiled at her son and agreed, "My Candelario is right. The Apache might come after us and our horses can go no further. We must ready ourselves. I, for one, will never be taken by them again!"

Felicia looked to her sister, and the women nodded and stood, holding their rifles before them. They looked to Candy and Felicia asked, "And where would you like us to go, Señor?"

Candy smiled at her use of the term for a man and looked at his mother, who also smiled but shrugged her shoulders, accepting him as the man in charge. He looked around and seeing several large boulders strewn about, he pointed at one on either side and the sisters each took one, then he pointed to another, somewhat closer, but smaller, he motioned for his mother to get down behind that one and said, "I will be here, by the horses. You three," raising his voice for the sisters to hear, "wait until they come near. They will look for you, for they do not want a niño, I will fall down, then you can shoot."

TATE COULD TELL by the tracks the horses had slowed, but he was pleased they had kept up the pace this far. Hopefully they would find a hiding place before the Apache could get to them. But his hopes were dashed when he heard a spattering of gunfire. He dug his heels into Shady's ribs, pulling the Spencer from the scabbard once again. He leaned far forward, the mane of the grulla slapping his face, and he saw Lobo stretching out beside them. Two more shots that Tate recognized as from a pistol, sounded. Within moments, he rounded the point of timber and saw two horses, obviously from the Apache, trailing their leads and trotting away. He looked in the direction from where they fled, and saw another horse standing and movement beyond. He pushed Shady on and stormed up on those in the small clearing. Sliding Shady to a stop, he swung a leg over the rump of the grulla and landed, rifle at the ready to see three women and Candy, standing, somewhat startled at his arrival and looking at him as if he were going to attack them. He looked around, saw three bodies of Apache lying sprawled in the dirt, unmoving. He looked back at the women and Candy said, "They," nodding toward the dead warriors, "didn't know who they were attacking." The women smiled, chuckled, and everyone dropped to the ground, tired and relieved.

CHAPTER TWENTY-TWO
STANTON

"Oh, you're hurt!" exclaimed Louisa, reaching her hand out toward Tate. She saw blood on his face and matted in his hair as he reached up to feel the side of his head. He winced at the touch and his fingers came away bloody. He looked at the woman as she came near and examined his wound. "How'd that happen?"

"Uh, there were some Apache back there that had it in their minds to kill me. One came purty close, I guess."

Louisa looked to her sister, "Can you find something to wash this with?"

Felicia looked around, then bent over to tear a strip from her petticoat, soaked it in water from the canteen, and handed it to her sister. "This'll hafta do, all we got!" she declared.

Louisa dabbed at the wound, finally leaning back and looked to Tate, "If that'd been any closer, you wouldn't be here."

"That happens on occasion," explained Tate, then looking around at the women, "If you ladies are up to it, maybe we can put a few more miles behind us, I think the short rest the horses had'll do 'em." In answer, each one fetched their horses and led them over to join up with Tate.

The trail was easy going, scattered juniper, cedar, and piñon made the trail move in and out of tree cover, but the terrain was reasonably flat and obstacle free. The horses ambled along at their own pace, Shady picking his own path as Tate dozed in the saddle. The shuffling gait made it easy to lapse into moments of reverie and idle speculation and Tate's thoughts turned to memories with family. But now the youngsters were no longer children, but he smiled at the thought that he and Maggie would have more time for themselves. He smiled at the image of his redhead, freckles parading across her nose, and dimples showing in her cheeks. They had been too long apart, and he was anxious to be home again.

"Is that it?" asked Candy, riding beside Tate and pointing ahead. The grey band of morning cast a dim light across the flats, making shadows stretch before drawing back on themselves. Tate looked where Candy pointed, "By jove, I think it is!" he answered smiling. He turned in his saddle and announced to the women, "Looks like we made it!"

The wide flat in the lee of the towering hill to the west, with scattered cottonwood and a few boxelder, held several seemingly out-of-place white stone and stucco buildings, many with pillared porches and gambrel roofs. A few were two-story and one with a cross at the front gable, had a high-pitched roof of wood shingles. Tate thought it looked like a small city with all the buildings built to match in style and color. But the women smiled at the sight of civilization, and Candy was excited, having never been to any settlement with more than three or four buildings.

Tate looked at the women, "First, I'll need to report in to the commandant. Then we should get us a place to stay, maybe let you ladies find a nice hot bath. I'm sure you'd like that."

The women smiled, laughing and chattering with one another. The commandant's office was in a separate building but sat near the sutler and Tate suggested the women go to the trader and find some new duds, "Tell the sutler I'll be along and settle the bill, just as soon as I finish with the commander. If he can direct you to a bathhouse, you go right ahead."

Tate stepped up on the portico, looking around and touching the columns, then opened the door into the entry. A corporal sat at a desk and looked up as Tate came near. "Yes?" he asked, scowling at the trail weary man. Tate realized it was probably a little early for visitors, but military posts usually started their day earlier than most settlements.

"I would like to see the commandant, if you please," asked Tate.

"And just what business would you have with the colonel?"

"I'm supposed to report in, I'm the scout for Colonel Carson," said Tate, somewhat disconcerted by the corporal's attitude.

"Do you have an appointment?" sneered the aide.

Tate leaned forward, putting his palms on the desk and looking directly at the blue boy and explained in firm but low tones, "I have orders from one colonel to another colonel. Nothin' 'bout my orders includes a boy with two stripes on his sleeves. So, I believe I would be within my rights if I found it necessary to clean my boots on your blue uniform if you don't fetch your colonel right quick."

With every word spoken, Tate leaned further forward, forcing the corporal to lean back until his chair hit the wall and the corporal considered climbing the wall to escape. But when Tate paused, he said, "Yessir, I'll tell the colonel you're here! Right away, sir!"

Tate leaned back, standing straight in front of the desk and letting a slow smile paint his face, "You do that."

The corporal jumped from his chair and scampered to the door and after a quick knock, entered. Tate could see him speaking to an older man seated at a desk, then spin on his heels and return to the outer foyer where Tate waited. "He'll see you now!" said the corporal, motioning to the door.

Tate walked to the desk, extended his hand to shake and said, "Colonel, I'm Tate Saint, scout for Colonel Carson."

The man behind the desk did not move nor take Tate's hand, but looked up at him and asked, "And just where is Colonel Carson?" The colonel, Joseph Rodman West, was a big man with full whiskers and hair that had retreated from the top of his head and now sat on his ears, scowled at the man before him with piercing eyes that showed from under thin eyebrows. He removed the stub of a well-chewed cigar from the tobacco stained whiskers and continued to stare at the Scout.

Tate stepped back, lowering his hand and put one hand on the back of a chair and crossed one foot over the other as he looked at the rude officer. After a short pause, Tate answered, "Oh, I reckon he'll be along any day now. Maybe today, tomorrow, or the next, depending."

"He was supposed to be here a week ago!" fumed the man. "I have orders to go to Fort McLane and take over there! Now, what kind of scout are you that you don't know where or when the colonel and his men will arrive?"

Tate casually sat down in the chair, took his hat off and smacked it against his leg to knock some of the dust off. He looked up at the colonel, "Well, it's like this. We've had to fight our way to get this far, and since I had three women and a boy with me, I didn't think I oughta backtrack an' put 'em in any more danger."

"Women?! What are you doing with women?"

"They was captives of some Mescalero an' it took me a while to convince Santana to let me have 'em. I don't know who them others were that tried to take 'em back, but no matter."

"Did you say Santana?"

"Ummhumm."

"How'd you know it was Santana?"

"He said so."

"Where'd you meet up with him?" asked the slightly exasperated colonel.

"Quivira."

"And?"

"And what?" asked Tate, enjoying the back-and-forth.

"What happened? And get to the point!" demanded the Colonel

"We left. That was, lemme see, three days ago. That was 'fore we ran into them others."

The colonel stood, aggravated, and motioned, "Get out of here! I've had enough of this!"

Tate slowly stood, "Who do I see 'bout quarters for the ladies?"

"Who are these women?" shouted the Colonel.

Tate answered softly, "They're the wives of some ranchers that were raided and killed. The women were taken captive by Santana and his band. But they've lost everything and could use some place to stay and recuperate 'fore we find some place for them to go."

"How'd you get them from the Apache?" asked the colonel, his voice now raised to almost a squeal.

"Killed 'em."

"You? You killed the Apache? How many were there?"

"Oh, 'bout a dozen or so."

The colonel dropped his eyes, shaking his head, and plopped down in his chair. "See the corporal there, tell him to get some officer's quarters for the ladies. Now, get out of my sight!" he growled, reaching for the stub of cigar in the ashtray.

Tate grinned, turned, and left the man's office. He looked to the corporal, "He's kinda touchy, ain't he?"

The corporal stifled a laugh and nodded his head as Tate added, "He said for you to get some officer's quarters for the ladies that are with me."

"What ladies?" he asked, looking toward the door.

"Three of 'em, and a boy that belongs to one of 'em. They're in the sutler's and also need a place for a bath."

The corporal looked up at Tate, then pulled out a list of the quarters, put his finger on one, then reached in the drawer for a key, "Unit D is available. That's the fourth one from the far end in that row," pointing out the window to the long row of adjoining units that marked the west edge of the garrison. "There's a bathhouse just beyond the sutler." Tate took the key and nodded his thanks as he opened the door to leave.

"DID YOU FIND EVERYTHING YOU NEED?" asked Tate as he walked toward the ladies, still looking around in the sutler's.

"Enough to make do," answered Felicia, as she looked to the others who were nodding their heads in agreement.

"Well, here's the key to your quarters." He turned to point out the officer's quarters, "It's unit D. Don't know what's there, but whatever you need, you just come back here and put it on account. Oh, and there's a bathhouse next door here, so you ladies should be fine, for a while at least."

"And where will you be?" asked Louisa.

"My favorite place. I'll be snoozin' on a big pile of hay in the loft of the stable," he declared, smiling. "Now, if you ladies will excuse me," he said, tipping his hat as he started for the counter to settle the account.

When the sutler stood before him, Tate asked, "You wouldn't have anyone that makes buckskins, wouldja?"

The man smiled and said, "We don't get much call for them, but yes, I have a Tiwa woman that makes a fine set, moccasins too. Beaded or not, however you want them. Might take a while, don't know what she has," he explained.

Tate grinned, "Fine, fine. Tell ya what I'll do, I'll get me some new duds here, an' drop off muh buckskins so she'll know what size I need 'em, and she can get to work makin' me a new set. Now, what do I owe ya' fer them ladies?"

The sutler showed Tate his scribblings of their purchases, added a figure for a set of clothes for him and a set of buckskins, then looked up at the man. Tate grinned, pulled a pouch from his belt and lay down three gold coins. "That'll cover whatchu got there and any more the ladies might need. We'll settle up the rest when I get ready to pull out. Fair 'nuff?"

"Yessir!" proclaimed the happy trader, quickly pocketing the coin.

It was mid-afternoon when a ruckus in the central compound woke Tate from his snooze in the loft of the stable. He looked out the haymow door and saw the arrival of Carson and his two companies of men as they ushered the almost four hundred Mescalero into the parade ground. Carson was barking orders and the officers were rushing about to carry them out, motioning to the Indians where to gather and wait. Tate leaned against the side of the big door that overlooked the entire area, chuckling at the melee as the tired bunch sought any place to stop and rest. Tate looked down when he heard a familiar voice, "Señor Tate! Señor Tate!" he called.

"Be right down, Candy. Hold on!" declared Tate as he went to his bedroll for his belt and hat. He scampered down the ladder and walked to the boy, "Now, what's all the excitement about, I thought you and the women were s'posed to be catchin' up on your sleep."

"Si, but they wanted me to find you and tell you to come to dinner later."

"Well, now. That sounds like an invitation I can't hardly refuse. You tell your ma that I'll surely be along. Oh, and tell her I might bring someone with me, if they don't mind."

"Oh, they won't mind, not Mamá, she likes to feed lots of people!" he declared, smiling. Tate looked down at the boy, "By the way, Candy, you look mighty fine in your new duds. How's them shoes workin' out for you?"

The boy smiled, touching his shirt to feel the material. "Fine, Señor. I never had shoes like these before," he proclaimed, sticking one out for inspection as he spoke.

They were interrupted when Carson rode up, "There you are! And who's your friend?" said the colonel as he stepped down from his mount. His two lieutenants came up behind him and dismounted, then one took the colonel's horse and went into the barn to stable the horses. Tate grinned at the colonel, then with a hand on Candy's shoulder, "This is Candelario Rodriguez, a friend of mine that came with me from back north a ways. He and his ma and three other ladies needed some company to get 'em here."

Carson reached out to shake Tate's hand and added, "When you said you'd leave sign if there was any trouble, I expected to see a stack o' rocks, or somethin' like that, but no, you left a trail of dead Apache!

We didn't have any trouble followin' you, all we had to do was follow the turkey buzzards! I thought you were tired of all the killin'!"

Tate dropped his eyes to the ground, stubbed his toe in the dirt, looked back up to Carson, smiling, "I still am, but, well, you know, things just kinda happen."

"How 'bout after I see the commandant, we get together, maybe have somethin' to eat?" asked Carson.

"Got just the thing. Candy here just invited me to join the ladies at their new quarters, an' I tol' 'em I'd probably bring a friend. How's that suit'cha?"

Kit smiled and nodded his head, "Can't even remember the last time I had a homecooked meal. Ain't no way I'd pass that up."

Tate nodded and said, "We'll be waitin' for ya' in unit D, yonder."

CHAPTER TWENTY-THREE
ORDERS

THE BENCH BESIDE SHADY'S STALL WASN'T COMFORTABLE BUT IT WAS suitable for the two friends to have a little privacy amidst all the activity of the rapidly changing fort. While Kit leaned forward with both elbows on his knees, Tate leaned back against the post, one foot on the bench and his elbow on that knee as he looked at his friend. He couldn't remember a time when he saw this man, who was known for his bravery and tenacity in the midst of the most adverse circumstances, so frustrated and disgruntled.

"It's like I suspected, Tate. All these West Pointers and self-appointed toy soldiers, all of 'em bucking for position and power no matter who they've got to step over or how many people have to shed their blood. You know, I don't like the way this round-up of the Mescalero has been handled and those blamed orders of Carleton to *kill all the men wherever and whenever you find them!* I've purty well decided to get shuck of the whole bunch of 'em, soon's I get these people to Bosque Redondo. I don't trust anybody else to do it, they'd just as soon kill 'em all!" He slapped his knee and sat back to look at his friend.

He turned toward the wide-open double doors that admitted the only light, a glaze coming over his eyes. Then twisting back to his friend, "See that bunch out there?" motioning to the assembling troop in the central compound. "That's Captain McCleave with his Company A, First California Volunteers. That's the advance party headin' to Fort McLane, Colonel West will follow with the rest of his troop. They believe they can catch up to Mangas and put a feather in the colonel's cap! Ever since Carleton was made Brigadier after he took credit for what Captain Roberts did against Mangas Coloradas and Cochise at Apache Pass, West's been trying to do him one better and capture Mangas."

Tate just shook his head and listened. He wanted no part of the politics within the ranks of the commanders, especially when so many were trying for glory and honor in the war back east, and most of those here in the west were hankering for promotions or at least transfers so they could garner some glory of their own. He looked at Kit, knowing he was upset, and asked, "You serious about gettin' out?"

"Yeah, yeah I am. You got me to thinkin' 'bout all this madness with the Mescalero and the way things have been goin'. And you also got me thinkin' 'bout Josefa and missin' my family. So, I reckon I'll be turnin' in my resignation at Fort Sumner, or at Fort Marcy, dependin' on everything, you know."

Tate asked, "So, what does that mean for me?"

Carson looked at him and answered, "One more job an' you're done."

"Oh?" asked Tate, knowing he had no obligation to anyone but Carson and that was just a handshake between friends.

"Couple years back, there was a gold strike down at Pinos Altos, the miners had a few run-ins with the Apache and there was a bunch o' Southern sympathizers that called themselves the Arizona Guards that helped 'em out. But the Confederates didn't know how good that gold strike was an' then after the little set to here in New Mexico territory with Sibley an' them, well the boys in butternut an' grey left for Texas. Now, those miners haven't had a chance to get their gold out 'til now. They've had an escort from Fort McLean until they get to Fort Craig. Now, that's where you come in."

"Me? What do I have to do with a bunch o' miners and such?"

"That gold's been contracted to the Union and what with all the Apache an' some o' the Navajo doin' what they been doin', well, all the boys in blue are kinda busy, all thanks to General Carleton and Colonel West."

"Yeah, so," prompted Tate.

"I reckon I can spare you three men, not in uniform, to help get those two wagons to Fort Union. I figger your penchant for traveling at night would make things a little safer for all concerned. Then we can meet up at my ranch in Taos, and Josefa will let you put on the feed bag."

"You want me, and three men, to do what you and your couple hundred soldiers couldn't do? To take wagons with gold through the same Apache country you had trouble gettin' through with all them soldiers. And you wanna make me a nursemaid to some knot-head miners?"

Carson grinned, dropped his head then lifted back up to smile at Tate, "Yup, that's about it."

"I think that uniform's fit too tight. It's cuttin' off the blood to your brain!" spat Tate, shaking his head at the suggestion. He looked at Carson, "Fort Craig to Fort Union? That's it, then I'm done and can go home?"

The grinning colonel chuckled, nodding his head, "Yup, but don't forget the invite to my ranch. I figger by my takin' the Mescalero to Fort Sumner, leaving Major Hostettler here, then we might get there 'bout the same time!"

"Do I get to pick the three?"

"Sure!"

Tate thought for a moment, "Kaniache, Sergeant McIntosh, and whoever the sergeant chooses."

"Done! When do you want to leave?"

"Probably in the morning. I need to say good-bye to the ladies."

. . .

THE SERGEANT STOOD every bit as tall as Tate and probably outweighed him by at least fifty pounds, none of it fat. But without the uniform and the armful of stripes and hash marks, he wasn't quite as intimidating. His handle-bar moustache curled up as he grinned watching Tate's reaction to the three men before him. Beside the Sergeant stood a man just as big, but dark as the midnight sky, with just a touch of grey above his ears that reminded Tate of wispy clouds floating above a foreboding thunderstorm. He answered to Hoback and Tate didn't bother asking where he got that name; not knowing the man nor how much it would take to set him off and with his girth and broad shoulders, massive arms and broad chest, the last thing Tate wanted to do was set him off.

Tate was confronted by the three when he led Shady from the stable, trailing a commandeered bay gelding pack-horse. He was surprised to see the men waiting for him, horses saddled and themselves already outfitted in gear and clothing bearing no resemblance to the blue uniforms they were used to wearing. As Tate looked from one to the other, he said, "Alright, so you're Mac, you're Hoback, and I think you know Kaniache here," nodding to the Ute scout. "Did anybody fill you in on this little detail?"

"Nosir, we were just told to report ready to ride and leave the soldier trappins' behind," answered the sergeant.

"Like I said, you're not sergeant, and I for durn sure ain't no officer so you call me Tate an' no yessir, no sir, salutin' stuff, got it?"

The big mustachioed man nodded his head, lips pursed and standing silent. Hoback and Kaniache nodded as well. Tate began, "Now, here's what we'll be doin'," and began to explain the detail to the men, knowing they deserved to know what they would be facing. When he finished, "Let's go to the sutler and stock up, an if there's anything you need, speak up."

Tate had quizzed Carson and any others that knew the country, including Rosa and the sisters, about the terrain west of Fort Stanton. He had heard of the horrors of that part of the wild desert, but after learning more about the Malpais and the Jornada del Muerto, he chose to avoid the volcanic cinders of the Malpais and the Journey or Day of the Dead as the desolate flatlands were known. Taking an extra day or two would be worth avoiding the disreputable desolation. Fighting Apache was bad enough without having to fight the very terrain they traveled as well. They headed out to the west and would go north when they passed the long line of mountains that shadowed the fort.

The talk around the campfire and during the rides in the night revealed much about the men Tate traveled with for this mission.

"Aye, me father's father was in the Fourth Royal Irish Dragoon Guards during the Napoleonic wars, and me Uncle Winn was a proud man in the Highland Scots. Both were often called true Gaelic Warriors. Now, me father, aye, he was an officer with the 88th Regiment of Foot, known as Connaught Rangers! They were such fearsome fighters they earned the nickname of "The Devil's Own!" He chuckled as he remembered the times of sitting before the cookfire in their modest home that sat on the glen in the country known as Connaught and listening to the tales of the men in his family and the battles they fought. He had determined at a young age that he would follow in the footsteps of his father and his father's father.

"Aye, but fate had a different course for me. So, when we left the homeland to come to America just as the blight on the potatoes began, it fell to me to carry on the tradition in America. And when I lost me family, Mum, Pa, and muh sister too, to the Cholera aboard ship, it was all that was left for me. As soon as we landed, I cornered the first man in uniform and joined up." He nodded his head, grinning, "but when I sobered up, I wondered if I had done the right thing, but there was no changin' it then!"

"And what about you, Hoback? What's your story?" asked Tate, stirring the gravy for the dutch oven biscuits. Since they had a packhorse, Tate had determined they would at least have the hardware and fixings to eat a little better on this trip. He looked to the big man who usually rode in silence and listened as the deep voice seemed to vibrate the very trees around them.

"Well, boss, I was borned a slave, muh mam and pap were slaves, and I was put in the field when I was big 'nuff to stand on muh own. Was sold two times, and growed up some, but the last massuh was a mean man and his overseer liked to beat the men and use the women, bad. When he wanted to lay the whip to me the last time, I took it from him and tolt him to never do that ag'in, then I showed him how it felt. Then I run away. Went to St. Louis, took to work on the docks as a stevedore, done the work o' three men an' the boss man liked what I done. When the slave catchers came after me, the boss man paid 'em off, and I worked even harder for him. When he was ready to quit workin', on 'count he was gettin' old, he give me muh manumission papers an' tol' me to either go to the mountains, or join the army. So I done it."

Neither Tate nor Mac moved all the while the big man spoke, and when he finished, they dropped their eyes to the fire, thinking about the man's life and what he had suffered, but their thoughts were interrupted when Hoback added, "That's where I gots muh name, when the army man saw my back, he said it looked like sumbuddy done took a hoe to it. But the army's been good to me. Got clothes, shoes, food, place to sleep, an' ain't nobody wanted to try to whip me."

Mac grinned, having known the man a couple years, chuckled and looked to Tate, "And I don't think anybody could whip him if they tried!" Both Tate and Hoback laughed at the thought and the mood lightened as the men readied their plates for a good meal.

CHAPTER TWENTY-FOUR
MINERS

FORT CRAIG WAS AN IMPOSING STRUCTURE, WITH HIGH GRAVEL bastions surrounding the stone buildings within, it was constructed for over two thousand troops. The largest fort in the southwest, it had been too daunting for the Confederates and General Sibley chose to bypass the fort, knowing he had neither the troops nor the artillery to lay siege. Tate looked at the fort on a slight knoll on the west bank of the Rio Grande, impressed by the number of cannons that lay atop the bastions. He and his men crossed over the wide river and went to the sally port. When hailed by a trooper, he reined up, leaned on the pommel and looked down at the young man.

"What's your business here?" demanded the trooper, holding his rifle across his chest.

Tate chuckled, "Ain't no business, just obeyin' orders, same as you. We're here to get them wagons yonder," nodding his head toward two wagons that sat before the sutler's with several men, obviously not soldiers, lazing about.

The trooper looked toward the wagons, then back to Tate, "Are you from Fort Stanton?" looking from Tate to the other three men, pausing as he looked at the Ute.

"That's right, orders from Colonel Carson."

"Go ahead, but report to headquarters, they've been waiting for you," instructed the trooper, stepping back to the edge of the big gate.

With a nod, Tate turned to the others and motioned for them to follow. As he stepped down from Shady, he looked around and paused as he visually examined the many cannon about the bastions. He looked to Mac, "What's with those cannon, somethin' ain't right."

Mac chuckled, "Most of 'em are what's called Quaker Cannon. They ain't nuthin' but carved wood with soldiers caps sittin' beside 'em. Those what ain't got caps, they're real. That's what kept Sibley from attacking back 'fore the battle of Valverde!" He chuckled again, and mumbled, "Dumb Rebels, ain't got no sense."

"WE EXPECTED AT LEAST a full squad, more like a full company, and he sends four men?!" sputtered Colonel Canby, commanding, standing behind his desk looking at Tate.

"Carson thought we might make it easier if we looked like miners 'stead of a bunch of soldiers. Course, he was prob'ly thinkin' he got most o' the Mescalero rounded up, some'eres 'bout four, five hunnert of 'em. He's takin' up to Gen'l Carleton up to Bosque Redondo. Then again, there's Mangas Coloradas, but word is he an' his three, four hunnert warriors were down south of here. So, I'm thinkin' he's thinkin' we might be able to slip through without much notice."

"Then it's going to be on him if you don't! I'm putting it in my report that I disagree with this nonsense, but Carson has Carleton's ear, so . . ." mumbled the colonel as he plopped back down in his chair. He looked up at Tate, "He must either have a lot of confidence in you and your men or else he just signed your death warrant."

"Well, I'm sure hopin' it ain't the latter!" snickered Tate, rising to leave. "Anything I should know 'fore we take on outta here, Colonel?"

The colonel leaned back in his chair, looked up at Tate, and with his hands together fingertips touching, "There are four men per wagon and each wagon trails two saddle horses. The men are armed with sidearms and Springfield rifles. Wagons have false bottoms that hold the gold, covered with usual miners' equipment. I think the men are capable miners, but I have no idea as to their fighting ability. They were escorted here by a company of mounted infantry from Fort McLean and they had no trouble. But . . . tell me, what about your men, any good?"

"I think so. Sergeant McIntosh and Corporal Hoback are proven. And Kaniache, a Ute scout and friend of Carson's, has proven himself as well."

At the mention of McIntosh, the colonel smiled, chuckled, and answered, "I know Mac and Hoback. Those two men are worth more'n a whole company of greenhorns." He looked long and hard at Tate, "And I s'pose, if Carson has confidence in you and the Indian, you just might make it."

"We're countin' on it, Colonel. I've got family waitin' for me an' I don't mean to disappoint 'em."

The colonel stood, extended his hand across his desk, and as the men shook hands, "Well, good luck, 'cause I believe you'll need it!"

"Thank you, sir," answered Tate and turned to leave.

TATE HAD SENT Mac to get the wagons and miners ready and as he neared the group, he saw the wagons were hitched to double teams and had been turned around, facing the big entry gate. Several men stood beside the wagons, with one grumpy-looking slouch sitting atop the first one and glaring at Tate as he neared. Tate stepped up on the boardwalk, looked toward the second wagon and saw it too had a driver mounted, but the others stood nearby in what appeared to be a stand-off with Mac, Hoback and Kaniache. As Tate stopped, he looked them over. The big man on the first wagon had scruffy whiskers, floppy hat, eyebrows almost as thick as his whiskers and joined in the middle, tobacco stains on his beard and shirtfront that stood open to show a broad and very hairy chest. He growled, "Are you the one they call Tate? You s'posed to be in charge of these?" motioning toward Tate's three men.

"That's right."

"I'm Bull! I'm the one in charge here, an' don't you forget it!" he growled, sticking one foot up on the foot-board of the wagon, "An' we ain't goin' nowhere with that Injun and that Nigra!"

Tate looked at the man, then to his men. He pointed to Hoback, jerked his thumb toward Bull, then to Mac and the other wagon. Both men grinned and walked toward the wagons. With a sudden grab, Hoback snatched Bull's foot from the board with one hand and jerked him from his seat with no more effort than pulling a weed. Bull grabbed at the side boards and leadlines, trying to hold on, but his head smacked on the footboard and Hoback swung the man around like he was spinning a rope over his head and let him fly. Bull hollered as he spun through the air, flailing his arms like a windmill, and landed flat of his face in the dust almost twenty feet from the wagon. The wind knocked out of his lungs, he gasped for air, trying to push himself up and coughing up dust, blood, and spittle. He rolled to his back and sat up, looking like a dirty rag doll as the men on the boardwalk stood still and stared.

Mac walked toward the second wagon, but the man quickly climbed down, holding his hands up in surrender and backing away to the group of miners now standing quiet on the boardwalk. Tate looked at the group and spoke softly, "Now, these wagons are going to Fort Union, with or without you. My orders are to get them and their contents to the fort and those orders don't say anything about you or that trash," he nodded toward the one called Bull, still spitting and gasping for air as he sat in the dirt. "I understand you men have not been paid for your cargo, and that pay is waiting in Fort Union. So, I suggest if you want to get paid, you will follow my orders and do as you're told. If you do, you just might make it to Fort Union. But if you want to follow that," another nod toward Bull, "then have a seat where you are and we'll wave to you as we leave."

The men looked at one another, then to Bull, and without any discussion, they mounted the wagons and took their places, ready to pull out. Tate nodded, went into the Sutler's to get some more coffee and beans, returned and mounted Shady and with a wave to Lobo, the men and wagons followed him from the fort. He noticed Bull had resumed his seat on the lead wagon but stared only at the rear end of the team before him, quiet all the while.

The sun was to their back when they rose from the wetlands on the east side of the Rio Grande. Just an hour out of Fort Craig, and with lowlands in the west cradling the golden orb, dusk was soon to settle across the land. Tate and Kaniache rode far to the front of the wagons, split wide apart while Mac and Hoback followed at the flanks of the wagons.

Tate knew the miners were wondering what they were doing so he dropped back beside the first wagon and spoke to Bull, "We'll be doin' our travelin' at night. Ya' might wanna spell each other at the drivin', but we'll stop to rest the horses now an' then and take a good break 'bout midnight. Don't be stoppin' till we give you the high sign, an' we'll pick out the cover."

"Ain't that kinda foolish, travelin' at night? Can't see nuthin' an' could break a axle or sumpin'," grumbled Bull.

"Long's you follow us, we'll keep you on a good trail and we won't break anything at night that wouldn't break in the daytime. With so few of us, it's best to stay outta sight of the Apache."

"You afraid o' the 'Pache?" growled Bull, snarling toward Tate, his resentment showing with the hatred in his eyes.

Tate looked at the man, his eyes squinting just slightly as they do when one was considering the object of their perusal, and responded, "Any man that knows 'em, fears 'em."

"Hah! Ain't no differ'nt any other Injuns. All of 'em are savages an' need to be kilt!"

Tate just shook his head at the man's inanity and gigged Shady away.

Bull hollered after him, "Don't worry, we'll protek'cha!" laughing at Tate's back.

Again, Tate shook his head, thinking, *If it wasn't for the rest of us, I'd almost as soon some Apache did attack, just to teach that bull-headed fool a lesson!*

TATE HAD PICKED a landmark in the better light of dusk, and as they neared the round-topped ridge set apart from the flat-topped butte, he directed the wagons to what he thought would be good cover for their midnight break. They dropped into the dry wash and rose to the saddle between the two land formations, pulling up near the steep slope of the butte and reined up to take a rest. Although it was to be a brief break, Tate had the men take the harnesses off the teams, letting them have a good roll and stretch and graze on the bunch-grass. Tate climbed to the top of the butte that rose over a hundred feet higher than the surrounding terrain, and with Lobo at his side, he scanned the territory ahead by the light of the stars and moon. The clear night offered a good view, but every clump of sage or grease wood showed as a shadow and the cholla stretched as black skeletons in the dim light. Tate knew only movement would tell of anything on the flats, and the empty plains kept their secrets well.

When he returned to the men, he was pleased to see Mac had used the talus slope from the ridge and the wagons to hide the small fire where the coffee brewed. The men had their stretch and were now reclined on the slight slope that offered nothing comfortable but at least stationary seats as they stared at the flames, lost in their own thoughts. Tate knew the men with the wagons were probably thinking of what they would do once they cashed in on the shipment of gold, but he wondered about Mac and Hoback. What were they looking forward to or did they have any thoughts of their future?

As he sat down near Mac, the man looked at him and asked, "See anything?"

"Nothin' movin' 'cept a couple coyotes chasin' some jackrabbits."

"That's good. Don't wanna see nuthin' bigger. Had 'nuff o' them 'pache!"

"You too?" asked Bull, looking at Mac. "I thought that'n was the only one that was skeered," nodding to Tate.

Mac looked sideways at the troublesome Bull, "I've been with that man for more'n a month now. Been through several fights, seen the leftovers from some of 'em, but I ain't never seen him scared."

Bull sat up, pushing out his chest in an effort to intimidate, "What kinda fights?"

"Just never you mind, boy," interjected Hoback, glaring at Bull and standing to go to the fire.

Bull leaned back, grumbling, but thought better of starting anything now. Maybe later.

CHAPTER TWENTY-FIVE
STORM

SHORTLY AFTER STARTING OFF AFTER THEIR MIDNIGHT BREAK, THE cloud cover began to dim the lights of the night. The milky way, or Path of the Ancients, was hidden and the quarter moon struggled to break through the darkening clouds. With three more hours of travel behind them, Tate was wondering about the weather as he watched jagged bolts of lightning search the terrain ahead with their bony fingers of white. The storm was moving in from the east, and the accompanying booms of thunder told Tate the tempest was about ten miles away. He used the lightning flashes to search for high ground, but none was near.

Arroyos, dry washes, and gullies scarred the desert flats, but offered no protection. To the west, the terrain dropped off to the wetlands and the Rio Grande, while further to the east there were buttes and plateaus aplenty, but they were fifteen to twenty miles away, too far to make cover before the storm hit. The sudden flash of lightning shadowed a slight knoll, but only for an instant. Tate turned Shady toward the last sighting and kicked him up to a canter. He didn't expect any danger in the flats, but any gulley or its like would likely be deadly with flash floods from the downpour. He reined up as he neared the knob, quickly searched out the few clusters of cedar and piñon, and satisfied, turned back to the wagons.

The wind had picked up and once the wagons were situated near the trees, horses picketed among the cluster, and a small fire kindled, the coffee began to perk its promises. The miners kept to the wagons while Kaniache and Tate built a lean-to for the four escorts. Facing the fire and well covered with layers of juniper branches and a canvas, it was a cozy spot for the four. But when the downpour began, the fire was quickly snuffed out and they pulled back into their shelter. Wrapped in blankets with Lobo at their feet, the men sat close, as close as men are wont to do, and thoughts turned to conversation.

"Got'ny family, Tate?" asked Mac.

"Ummhumm, wife and two young'uns. Well, they were young, but the boy's got him a wife now and the daughter, well, she's growed up but still t'home," answered Tate, a glaze coming over his eyes. "How 'boutchu, Mac?"

"Nope, though I come close once. Army life just ain't very appealing to most lassies. But, maybe after the war's o'er, an' if I get back east where the women are, I might find me a willing wife," grinned Mac. He looked to Hoback, "How 'bout'chu, Hoback? I dinna remember you ever speakin' of a woman."

The big man looked at the others, grinning, "Had me a woman once, but the massa sold her. Tried to find her, but she was too long gone. Thought about findin' me a native woman, though. They say they have a likin' for men like me," answered Hoback, lifting his eyes to the downpour and stretching out a hand to feel the rain.

Tate chuckled, "You know, that's true. The native women tend to look at a man for what kind of children he might have, and they favor big, strong, and brave men. I knew a man a while back, up in the Absaroka Mountains, like you, he was a former slave, freed by his owner, but fell in with some bad men and lost his woman. His name was Caleb, but the Indians called him Black Bear. And when he met up with a Shoshoni Medicine woman, called Stands Like a Bear, he met his match, and far's I know, they're still together."

"Good life?" asked Hoback, eyebrows lifted expectantly.

"Good life! He fit right in with the warrior society, he's a good hunter, his father-in-law, the chief, likes him. Yeah, he's got a good life!" answered Tate, remembering his friend. Tate looked to the Ute, "What about you, Kaniache? You got a woman?"

The stoic man looked at Tate and the others, let a slow smile tug at the corners of his mouth, and answered, "Two."

The other three men snapped their heads around to look at the scout who sat on their left, his back to the side of the lean-to. He was smiling, "Four children, three girls one boy. Tipi crowded, so when Carson asked for me, I came."

The other three men laughed, and Tate said, "That bad?"

"That good, always tired, but need time away to rest," answered the man, still grinning.

Hoback looked at Kaniache, "So, it's alright for a man to have more than one wife among your people?"

Kaniache nodded his head, "But must provide for them. More hunting, more work."

Hoback grinned, "Now I know I wanna find a native woman, or two!" he declared.

"As long as they're not Apache," exclaimed Tate.

IT WAS mid-morning before the rain let up, leaving behind puddles and mud holes across the flats. Every gulley and wash ran high with muddy water and debris, but with no nearby mountains, Tate knew the run-off would soon diminish into trickles and the warm summer sun would quickly return the desert to its dry land habitat. But travel in the wet adobe was impossible, for every step of the horses would build up the slick clay on their hooves and make each step hazardous. Tate climbed to the top of the slight knoll and found a seat on a sand-stone slab and pulled out his scope for a good scan. Unable to travel in the daylight, he hoped the sun would work to their advantage and dry things out enough so they could resume their trip at dusk. But only time would tell, and he knew they had to be on guard against any possible sighting by the Apache.

With a quick look around, Tate saw exactly what he expected: nothing. Satisfied, he returned the scope to its case and withdrew his Bible for his time with the Lord. He grinned as he remembered the words of his father, "Son, when you pray, that's you talking to God. When you read the Bible, that's God talking to you. So, which do you think is more important, what God says or what you say?" Those had been words that had guided Tate time and again as he spent time with the Lord and when he was tempted to just pour out his heart to God, he remembered that God had already poured out His heart for him.

He finished his reading with Proverbs 3:5-6, *Trust in the Lord with all thine heart; and lean not unto thine own understanding. In all thy ways acknowledge Him, and He shall direct thy paths.* He smiled, thinking that was exactly what he needed, was for God to direct his paths. As he closed the Bible, he heard the rattle of stones and looked to see the big man Hoback coming to the top of the knoll.

"Alright if'n I come up?" asked the big man.

"Sure!" answered Tate, moving to the far side of the big sandstone slab, offering Hoback a seat on the stone.

Hoback sat down, looked off in the distance, then turned to see the colors of the sunrise painting the drifting clouds with pinks and oranges. He smiled at the display of beauty even here in the desolate reaches of nowhere and turned to Tate. "I seen ya do this a'fore, when we was with Carson. You know, coming away with your Bible an such, an' I wondered."

"Wondered? What did you wonder about, Hoback," asked Tate, curious about the big man.

"Well, muh mam was a spiritual woman, an was always talkin' 'bout God and such. She prayed and learned to read, just so's she could read the Book. An' she was always wantin' me to be like her, but I couldn't do it. I was mad plumb through, all the time. An' it seemed like ever time I started listenin' to muh mam, or muh pap, then the overseer'd get after me, an' I'd take another whippin'. Seemed like God didn't want me, and even that made me mad!" He hung his head for a moment before continuing. "Then when Mam was on her death bed, she helt muh han' an' made me promise to learn to read an' learn 'bout God. She wanted me to go to Heaven like she was, but . . ." and again, he dropped his head. He wiped a tear from his eye and looked to Tate, "I ain't done what I promised."

Tate sat silent, waiting, then asked, "Do you want to? I mean, do what you promised?"

Hoback looked up, "Yassuh, more'n anythin'. Could you he'p me?"

Tate grinned, "I'd be glad to, and tell ya' what, how 'bout we start right now?"

Hoback again wiped away a tear and nodded his head enthusiastically, smiling broadly.

Tate flipped through a few pages, stopped and pointed, "First thing to get settled is your promise about Heaven. Now look here," then looking to Hoback, "can you read?"

"Some, but it's hard," answered the man, looking to Tate.

"Well, here in John 3:3, Jesus said, *Except a man be born again, he cannot see the kingdom of God.*" The big man looked at Tate, brow furrowing, showing he didn't understand. Tate continued, "To be born again, is what the book of Romans describes as being saved from eternal death. Here's what you need to know. There are a few things to understand, first, Romans 3:10 says *There is none righteous, no not one.* See Hoback, that means we, you and me and everyone else, we are sinners. Understand?"

"Yessuh, I'm a sinner, I know that!" he nodded his head.

"Then Romans 6:23 says *The wages of sin is death,* which means because we're sinners, we're doomed to death. And that's not just dying, that's eternal death in hell. But, the rest of the verse says, *but the gift of God is eternal life through Jesus Christ our Lord.* See, Hoback, God loves us, and even though we're deserving of death and hell forever, He gave us a gift of eternal life and he purchased that gift when He died on the cross for our sins. Romans 5:8 tells us that. But like any gift, we have to accept it for it to be ours. That's what your Mama wanted you to do, accept that gift."

"But, how do I do that, boss?" asked Hoback.

Tate smiled, "That's the easy part. But, you can't do it unless you absolutely believe it with your whole heart. See, here in Romans 10:9 it starts off, *That if thou shalt confess with thy mouth the Lord Jesus and believe in thine heart that God hath raised him from the dead, thou shalt be saved. For with the heart,* and that's what I meant when I said you have to believe it with your whole heart, you can't just try it out to see if you like it, *with the heart, man believeth unto righteousness and with the mouth confession is made unto salvation.* And on down in verse 13, *For whosoever shall call upon the name of the Lord, shall be saved.*

"See, my friend. It's that simple. God made it simple so everyone could understand it. We're sinners, we deserve hell forever, but God bought us the free gift of eternal life, and all we have to do is accept it, believing with our whole heart, and we will have it. That, my friend, is life eternal in Heaven with God and your mother. Would you like to do that?"

Hoback hung his head again, then lifted his tear-filled eyes to Tate, "Yassuh, I would."

Tate led the big man in a simple prayer, asking God's forgiveness and asking for the free gift of eternal life. When the amens were said, Hoback lifted his face, smiling and reached out to shake Tate's hand. Tate looked down to see his hand disappear in the big ham-hock fist of Hoback and grinned, as Hoback said, "Thank you, thank you."

Tate looked from the man to the distance, saw the clouds disappearing and the sun rising, then said, "I think I smell breakfast. How 'bout we go get somethin' to eat?"

CHAPTER TWENTY-SIX
FIGHT

AFTER TRAVELING MOST OF THE NIGHT AND WITH THE TRAIL AHEAD A continuous mudhole, there was no argument given when it was suggested to get more sleep. The unwashed miners didn't seem to mind sharing the wagons with one another, and the escorts were happy to breath fresh air as they stretched out under the lean-to. But Tate had other things in mind and found a solitary spot for his bedroll, under the big juniper that climbed the slope behind them. Lobo provided company and shared the shade, resting his chin on Tate's ankles.

Just past mid-day, Tate heard stirring near the wagons and both he and Lobo lifted their heads to look below the branches of the cluster of trees and saw the legs of teams and trailing of harness. He rose, picking up his bedroll and rifle and walked back to the camp. Bull and three of the miners were harnessing and hitching up the horses. The other four were busy at a blazing campfire, cooking up a meal and some coffee. They were neither quiet nor concerned, the fire giving off a pillar of smoke that could be seen for miles.

Tate shook his head as he approached the group, "What's goin' on?" he asked, having already guessed who was behind the ruckus.

Bull turned around, "We're pullin' out, tired o' sleepin' an' waitin' on you soljer boys! Sun's out, trail's dried, an the sooner we get to Fort Union, the sooner we get paid! So, we're travelin'!" he declared, standing with his arms folded across his chest, glaring at Tate.

Lobo leaned against Tate's leg and let a low growl rumble from his chest, showing his teeth as he stared at the man. Tate spoke softly, "Easy boy, not yet."

"I told you I'm the boss o' this outfit, an' I'm sayin' we're goin' an' there ain't nuthin' you can do 'bout it!" snarled Bull, "An' if'n you know what's good for you, you'll keep that mutt back or I might have to kill both of ya."

Tate sensed rather than heard Kaniache and Hoback behind him, and Mac stepped beside him. Tate asked, "What about the Apache?"

"What Apache? We ain't seen no 'Pache an' the only Injun is that'n behind you!"

"Well, Bull. Here's how it's gonna go. If you and your men want to leave, you can take those four saddle horses and skedaddle. But, the wagons an' what's in 'em are stayin' with us," declared Tate without any bluster, just standing, feet apart and hands at his sides.

Bull grinned, dropped his arms and snarled, "You think you can stop us?"

"Yup."

Tate turned slightly to speak to Hoback and Mac, "You two get the teams back from the wagons, unharness 'em and picket 'em. If those fellas give you any trouble, feel free to shoot 'em." The two big men grinned and started for the teams, the other miners backed away, none as ready to try to interfere with Mac and Hoback as Bull. "As for you Bull, why don't you just come over here so we can tend to business and not spook the horses?" He grinned as he motioned to Bull to come closer.

The big man grinned, thinking he would have an easy time with Tate. What he saw was a man a bit older and about twenty to thirty pounds lighter. Nothing about Tate impressed Bull, whose confidence was in his size and brute strength. He had many fights on the wharfs of West Port and before that when he worked as a hoggee on the Erie

Canal. There a man had to fight for rights of way on the canal and he was known as a dirty fighter. He growled as he started for Tate, arms spread and in a slight crouch, he was slobbering in anticipation, reminding Tate of his encounters with grizzly bears.

When Bull lunged for him, Tate sidestepped and went under the man's big arm, bringing his own fist up from the ground and burying it in the man's gut. Tate quickly stepped around the gasping and surprised Bull who staggered forward, hand at his middle and sucking air. He whirled around and his eyes grew large and mad, and he stomped toward Tate again, this time showing caution, but determined to destroy his opponent. Tate held his hands loosely at his side, watching the man's eyes, knowing they would give away his moves, and when they flared again, Tate struck with a left jab that rocked Bull's head back and followed it with a roundhouse right that split his cheek and bloodied his nose. Bull staggered back, wiping at his face and seeing his hand come away bloody, he glared at Tate, seeing no marks, or blood and his anger flared.

Bull charged again and Tate tried to sidestep, but Bull anticipated it and wrapped his big arms around him and snatched him off the ground as he bellowed, "I'm gonna break yore back!" and squeezed for all he was worth. Tate struggled for air, trying to squirm free, his arms pinned to his side, but the bulk of the man and the strength of his arms, began to crush the life from him. His eyes began to glaze, and he knew he was going to pass out if he didn't do something. Tate reared his head back and bashed his forehead against Bull's face, smashing his nose and lips and Tate heard the crack of a broken tooth. Bull roared but relaxed his grip and Tate pushed free. He fell backwards, gasping for breath as Bull stood, hands covering his face. As Tate rose, the beast of an angered monster called Bull roared so loud, it would have shamed the biggest bear in the woods and charged. Tate spread his feet wide, dropped into a crouch, and watched Bull's eyes. He knew the man expected him to try to sidestep, and Tate moved his arms wide. When Bull was just a step away, Tate lunged at his middle, burying his head in the man's solar plexus, grabbed his tree-stump legs and lifted him off the ground, driving him to his back with a thud that felt like an earthquake. Tate quickly went to his feet, standing over Bull, who, with the air knocked from him, tried to roll to his side. He started to come up on all fours, but Tate met him with a blow that came from his feet in an uppercut that smashed into his already obliterated face, lifting Bull off the ground, and the man dropped on his face in the dirt, barely breathing, but unconscious.

Tate stepped back, rubbing his knuckles, dropped his hands to his knees and struggled for air. None of the men moved, until a shout from above the trees, "Apache!" The warning was from Kaniache, who, seeing the smoke from the fire and the noise from the crowd, had climbed the slope to watch the surroundings. Now he slid down the hillside, pointing to the east, "Eight, ten, riding fast. They saw the smoke!"

"They'll be after the horses, get 'em back in the trees!" shouted Tate, then turning to the other men, "Get in the wagons! Get your rifles!" To Mac and Hoback, "There, in the rocks!" pointing to the stack at the base of the talus. He ran to his pile of gear, snatched up his rifle and bag with the cartridges, and scampered up the slope above the camp. He dropped behind a granite boulder just shy of the crest of the knoll, and once situated, searched the area to the east for the attackers. He had bellied down to look over the crest of the knoll and now saw the approaching Apache but was surprised when one rose right in front of him. They spotted each other at the same time and the Apache reacted first, charging with his tomahawk raised. Tate acted without a conscious thought, grabbing the big Bowie from the sheath between his shoulders and threw it in one deft motion. The blade reflected the sunlight in one quick flash before burying itself in the man's chest. The sudden strike startled the Indian and he hesitated in his steps, looked down to see the haft of the knife at his chest, lifted his frightened eyes to Tate, and fell forward, driving the knife deeper. His leg spasmed then he lay lifeless.

Tate quickly looked to the charging band, shouted to the others, "They split! Comin' round both sides!" He twisted around, on his knees behind the boulder, and searched right and left for his first target.

In an instant, they came on his left and he lowered the muzzle, following the first with his sights and quickly squeezed off his first shot. The Spencer roared and belched smoke as it bucked in his hands, but he was already jacking another shell into the chamber. He eared back the hammer as he followed another Apache, and again the Spencer bellowed. He heard the other rifles chatter as the men below were finding targets from both sides.

With eight miners and four escorts, the firepower was deadly and withering. The Apache, suffering several losses on their first attack, quickly withdrew behind the knoll. Tate crawled to the top, and saw there were only five, one obviously wounded, as they gathered together, thinking themselves out of range and sight of the white men. One man was shouting and gesturing as Tate took sight on him, believing him to be the leader, within seconds, the Spencer blasted the man from his horse and the others shouted, some screaming their war cries, but all dug heels to their mounts and fled.

When Tate saw the rest of the Apache fleeing, he vaulted down the slope to join the others, "Get the teams hitched, we're movin' out 'fore they come back with more!" The men scampered around, each finding a task and within moments, the wagons were readied, the saddle horses tied off behind, and the four escorts were mounted. As Tate and Kaniache led out, Lobo loped ahead on the trail, tongue lolling, happy to be moving. As Tate looked to the west, he calculated no more than an hour of daylight before dusk, then good light for another half hour to an hour before night dropped its curtain. They should be at least five or six miles away by that time, far enough to slow their pace and keep moving. He was confident they would do well this night, even with the bloody bulk of Bull in the back of the last wagon.

IT WAS near midnight when a well-traveled trail offered an easy way to the Rio Grande and water and graze for the horses. As they came to a thicket of willows and alders, Tate motioned the wagons to pull to the side of the trail beside the brush and unharness the horses. They took the opportunity for some fresh coffee and a bit of jerky. When Tate heard some groaning from the back of the wagon, he went to the tailgate and peered in at the crumpled form of Bull, tossing in some blankets in the dark.

"Bull?" called Tate.

"Yeah. What?" he growled.

"You've got a choice to make."

"What'chu mean?" he asked.

"We're just across the river from what I think is Socorro. It ain't much, but it's a town of sorts. We can leave you here with a horse and your gear, or, you can stay with us. But, if you stay, I want your word that you'll abide by my orders and not cause any more trouble. So, what's your choice?"

"You'd take muh word?" he asked, voice sounding doubtful.

"Yeah, I would."

Tate could hear the man breathing heavy in the dark, he groaned as he tried to move around, and Tate added, "But, you'll need to get on your feet and do your share."

Another heavy breath and a groan, then, "Alright. I'll give ya' muh word, an' I'll do muh share," he grumbled. He moved around in the wagon box, and Tate could tell he was scooting toward the tail gate. Tate stepped back, giving the man room to step down from the wagon. They walked to the fire together, saying nothing, but when the man came into the firelight, the men waiting there couldn't help but gasp as they looked at the bloody pulp of the man's face. When Tate looked, he grimaced, then turned to the other miners, "Any of you got'ny experience doctorin'?"

They looked to one another, each shaking their head, then Tate looked to Mac and Hoback. The big black man said, "I do, boss. But I ain't gonna touch that man. If I do, I'se liable to kill him!"

Mac chuckled, "I can take care of 'im, Tate. I done muh share with wounded men." Tate tossed him a satchel from the pack horse that had some bandages and ointments garnered from the sutler, then poured himself and Bull a cup of coffee. The worst of the man's damages were his face, but once cleaned up, the swelling and bruising and bandages gave the man a bit of a gruesome look, but fortunately there were no mirrors around.

"We've got a long way to go, so let's get movin'," ordered Tate as he and Kaniache once again took the lead. It was a cloudless night and the stars tried to outshine the moon but were unsuccessful in their attempt as the moon waxed toward full. Tate listened to a nighthawk, grinned at the voice of his feathered friend, and waited for the ever-present coyote to start his song of romance. But this night the mischief-maker of the desert was silent, surrendering his part in the symphony of the darkness to the frogs in the wetlands by the river and the cicadas in the flats with the crickets. It was music that Tate enjoyed.

CHAPTER TWENTY-SEVEN
BULL

Bull was gone. When they left the Rio Grande, four days ago, they had traveled east north-east toward the Manzanita Mountains. Tate led them through the break well north of the Jornada del Muerto, but it was still desert travel. Once across the break, he knew there would be water at the Quaria ruins, where they stopped with Carson. His goal after that was to retrace the route used by Carson and company when they started the round up of the Mescalero. Now they were about two days east of Albuquerque and two days due south of Santa Fe, headed for Las Vegas and Fort Union, about another three days, or nights, travel.

It was late afternoon when they discovered Bull had taken one of the saddle horses, a few supplies, and his gear. But once it was known he was gone, they took a count of the bags of placer gold and discovered only one bag missing.

"I don't understand it, Tate. His share was more'n one bag, an' it ain't like him to not take more'n his share!" stated Otis Flannery, the elder statesman of the remaining miners. He had gained the reputation and nickname of Professor when it was discovered he had been a professor of history at Brown University in Rhode Island, until he was stricken with gold fever.

"When you talked the last couple days, did he talk about anything in particular?" asked Tate.

"Well, we all kinda talked about what we were gonna do with the money we were getting. You know, dreams of big houses, and such. But all he could talk about was goin' to California. Said he wanted to get away from everything and everyone. He did say he wished he had more comin' to him. But all of us worked hard the last two years just to get what we got. Maybe he was wantin' to try his luck in the gold fields in California?"

Tate considered Otis' comments for a moment, then added, "The one time we talked, which was just last night 'fore we camped, he was actin' like we were old friends and all, but he kept askin' 'bout where we were, you know, what towns and such were where. When I told him the closest towns were 'bout the same distance, Santa Fe and Albuquerque, he just grinned and nodded his head. I guess he was plannin' sumpin' then, but what?"

Two other miners had joined them and heard the last of the conversation and one man, known as Knickerbocker, said, "I never did trust that man. He tried to short me one time when we were baggin' things up. Ya say he only took one bag o' gold?"

Otis answered, "That's right, just one. His share was more'n that!"

"That's it then, he's gonna do it!" responded Knickerbocker, slamming his fist into his palm.

"What'dya mean? What's he gonna do?" asked Tate, the others looking at the man.

Dropping his head and shaking it side to side, "He tried to get me to go in with him 'fore we left our diggin's. He said we could work together, take all the gold from the rest of you and shag out to California an' nobody'd ever know. He said if we kilt you in the night, we'd be long gone and a lot richer come mornin'. I tol' him he was crazy, I weren't gonna do it! Then he tried to make out he was just kiddin' anyway, but I knew he wasn't. After we contracted with the army, he never mentioned it again. Now, less'n I miss my guess, he's gone off to get some help an' he'll be back for all the gold, not just his share. He just took one bag so we wouldn't follow him and to show the others, whoever he gets, what might be waitin' for 'em."

Otis looked at the others, then to Tate, "That sounds like somethin' he'd do alright. The only reason his share was equal to the rest was because his partner was killed when a flume collapsed on him, leastways that's what he said, but no one else saw it." The others nodded in agreement and remembrance, and it was easy for Tate to see they all thought the same thing, that Bull had done his partner in intentionally.

"So, what do you think we oughta do, Tate?" asked Knickerbocker.

"I'm not sure just yet, but I'll be thinkin' on it. For right now, let's get hitched up on on the move."

IT WAS near midnight when Tate called a halt. They were well into the area called the flat-tops, near where Mangas Coloradas first laid the ambush for Carson that was thwarted by Tate's discovery. As they reined up, Tate gathered the men around to detail the plan he developed while they rode. "This is what I'm thinkin'. Bull's not much of a tracker or anything of the sort, so he'll prob'ly try to find one. And he'll think he knows where we're goin', so we'll just have to confuse him on that issue as well. So, here's what we'll do, after we get a bit of a rest here, have some coffee an' such, then we'll . . ." and he carefully detailed his plan, drawing a crude map in the dirt at his feet, making sure each man understood what would be expected of them. As he detailed his plan, the men slowly nodded their heads and began to grin as they understood. When Tate finished, "Any questions?"

"Yeah, how long ya figger it'll take us to meet up at, where was that, Las Vegas?" asked one of the miners that had not said much before. He was the one called Dutch, a big broad-shouldered man with cropped blonde hair and a ready smile.

"We're 'bout three days, mebbe a little more, from Fort Union, and Las Vegas is 'bout halfway," answered Tate. "There's a trader there that'll be a good place to meet up."

"An' you say, you're gonna hang back an' try to discourage 'em a little?" asked Otis, or Professor.

"Yup, we will," grinned Tate as he answered.

"We?" queried the professor.

"Ummhumm, I figger you'll be with me."

As planned, the two wagons were driven into two different arroyos, as far as possible and then covered with brush to try to hide them as well as could be done. The teams were driven out and everyone joined up again. The gold had been off-loaded and some of the equipment, which was now dispersed among the four groups. Mac, Hoback, Kaniache, and Tate would each lead a group of two miners and one pack horse, with Tate and the professor having the original pack horse used by Tate and company, and one of the team as the second. The gold had been evenly divided, and each group would take a different route, trying to obscure their trail as they traveled, but making the best time possible.

Mac and Dutch and his partner took the first arroyo to the north, then were to move across the flat tops through the upper end of the Cañon de los Diegos, bearing to the north-east toward the Pecos river. Hoback and Knickerbocker and his partner would also head north, taking a different arroyo further north of the route chosen by Mac, cross the Cañon Agua del Corral, and continue to the Pecos. Kaniache would have the longest and most difficult route, over the flat-tops to the south, bearing to the north-east past the site of the ambush against Carson and on toward the southern reaches of the Pecos, eventually to come out below Arroyo del Pueblo and on to Las Vegas. Tate and Otis would remain nearer the wide basin and would try to discourage Bull and company.

Once the others left, Tate looked to Otis, "Let's get up on top of that mesa yonder," nodding his head in the direction of a shoulder of the flat-top that jutted out into the wide valley, "an' you can keep a watch out for Bull an' comp'ny. I'll do a little work to try to cover the tracks of the wagons, at least 'nuff to confuse 'em a mite, and then I'll join up with you."

"Wouldn't it be better if I helped you? You can show me what to do, and I'm a purty good learner!" declared the professor, grinning.

"Alright, then." They tethered the pack horses, giving them enough lead to reach some bunch grass, then started out toward the first canon of the wagons. Tate explained, "We won't be able to completely hide all sign, but if we just use some juniper branches, brush out the tracks like this," explained Tate, using the branch like a big broom, moving it lightly and side to side, "then we'll dust that out by scattering some light soil by hand, like this," letting the loose soil drop from about shoulder high with the slight breeze scattering it throughout, "then it'll look more natural."

They worked at the first trail from the valley floor up the narrow arroyo about eighty yards and obscuring their own tracks as they backed out of the canyon, they turned to the second, repeating the process. It was nearing daylight when they finished their work on each of the tracks of the wagons and the four parties of men. When they rose to the crest of the mesa chosen before, the professor asked, "Do you really think that'll fool 'em?"

"Nope. But it might just confuse 'em. Maybe keep 'em busy and give the rest of the men a little extra time to get away. If they have any kind of a tracker with 'em, he might figger out what we're doin' but he won't know which trail to take. What I'm countin' on is Bull's greed that'll keep him from recruitin' too many men that he'd have to split the gold too many ways."

The professor let a slow smile paint his face, "And after all that, then you'll slow 'em down even more. But how are you going to do that?"

Tate slapped the stock of his Spencer and grinned, "They usually get discouraged when the Spencer here starts talkin'!"

CHAPTER TWENTY-EIGHT
DISCOURAGEMENT

TATE SURRENDERED THE WATCH DUTY TO OTIS, STRETCHED OUT AND pulled the hat over his eyes to keep out the rising sun, and sought to doze a little. Lobo was at his side and Tate had confidence in his long-time companion to warn him of any danger, as would Shady, standing three-legged on the dark side of a lone juniper. The professor was elbow down on the big sandstone slab, using Tate's telescope to watch the valley for the approach of Bull and company. Although they weren't certain that Bull was going to come, the other miners were agreed he would try for the entire shipment of the gold.

It was mid-morning, and Tate and Otis had switched off watching when Lobo jumped with front feet on the sandstone and started toward the valley floor, ears forward and eyes appearing to squint. Tate swung the scope in the direction the wolf was looking and first spotted a bit of dust, then several mounted men. As he watched, he easily recognized the big Bull in the lead, then counted five other men, all appearing to be Mexican, with him. He stretched out a foot to nudge Otis awake, but never took his eyes off the riders.

He knew the approximate location where they had wiped out the wagon tracks and waited as they approached. Suddenly, Bull reined up, leaning to the side, and Tate chuckled, "They've found where the wagon tracks disappear," he spoke softly to Otis. The end of the sandstone slab where Otis knelt, rested against a gnarled cedar trunk with a lone branch of blue bristled cedar living. The twisted grey trunk futilely clawed at the distant heavens, casting a distorted shadow across the slab and Otis.

"How many?" asked the professor.

"Five, plus Bull." He watched as Bull and two others dismounted to search for the tracks of the wagons. The big man stood, shading his eyes as he searched farther down the valley, then turned to look at the many canyons and arroyos that came from the flat tops. The two other men, apparently the trackers, were moving about, walking in a wide circle, searching for sign. Bull was waving his hands at the others, probably shouting, and the others dismounted and started searching for tracks also. As the men moved about in wider and wider circles, finally one of them shouted and waved, indicating he had found some sign. Tate grinned, remembering where he intentionally left a track untouched, wanting them to go into the canyon where the first wagon was hidden. He chuckled, "They took the bait," laughing, he looked to the professor. "Now, they'll all go rushing up there, trying to find us, but we won't be there!"

Tate twisted around, sat down with his back to the stone, and laughed, "I can just see that Bull, he'll be grinnin' like a coyote in a chicken coop, thinkin' he's got us cornered. He'll send the men, some on both slopes of the arroyo, tryin' to sneak up, certain we'll be sleepin' off the night's travel. It'll take 'em a while to find it," he chuckled again, picturing the action as he described it, "but when they do, Bull will have 'em open up and shoot the daylights outta the wagon an' them blankets we put under the trees. Then when there's no return fire, they'll slowly walk up, probably shoot the blankets again, then they'll hafta search the wagon. They'll tear it apart cuz of that false bottom, an' the more they work at it, the madder Bull's gonna get!" Both Tate and the professor laughed at his description, knowing that would probably be exactly what Bull would do, and he would be mad!

They came out of the arroyo on the run, Bull barking orders and waving his arms as the men scattered, looking for more tracks. It was all of a half hour before the signal was given from the mouth of the second arroyo. The men followed their tracker at a canter, guns ready, and Tate and Otis, sat chuckling at the spectacle. The men were closer to their promontory now, but still too far away to understand what was being said, but a little imagination was sufficient for Tate and the professor to share a laugh. As the band of thieves disappeared into the canyon, Tate looked to Otis, "Mac and his bunch took off up that first arroyo, so Bull never saw their sign, and it looks like they got away clean. Now, this draw below us is where Hoback and his men went. I'm countin' on Bull's men to find some sign and wanna start after him, but that's where it'll get interestin'. Now, if they split and some of 'em go 'round this point, I'm countin' on you to mis-direct 'em a little. Reckon you can do that, Professor?"

"Well, I'm not a crack shot, but I can usually hit what I'm aimin' at, so, yeah, I can probably mis-direct them a mite," answered the professor, catching the mischievous mood of Tate.

They heard the ratcheting gunfire from the second arroyo, telling them the men had found the second wagon. Tate chuckled again as he pictured Bull's anger beginning to boil over. He knew the man was big, but it was also evident he wasn't the smartest miner he ever met. As is often true with men that rely on their bulk instead of their brain, Bull had made it this far in life bullying others and bending their will to his by sheer force. But when might doesn't make right, conflict usually rages. As the gunfire subsided, Tate picked up his rifle, motioned for Lobo to follow, and trotted along the edge of the rimrock atop the mesa, working his way further up the canyon. He spotted another rocky edge and lowered himself to look over and back up the draw. Satisfied with his choice, he bellied down and readied himself, laying the Spencer across the granite rock, with an extra tube of cartridges alongside.

By now, Bull had wasted more than a couple hours, chasing tracks and searching for his fellow miners and the gold, all to no avail. Tate knew his hired bandidos were probably getting a little aggravated with this gringo and the tension was rising, both among the would-be thieves and Tate and Otis as well.

A single gunshot sounded near the mouth of the draw, Tate guessed it to be a signal, and pulled the Spencer to his shoulder. The men, all of them, were following Bull and the tracker as they walked their mounts up the gravel bottomed canyon, several leaning over to search for sign. The tracker pointed, swung down from his saddle and was joined by Bull. The tracker fingered the tracks, pointing to the brush marks and sand, and Tate heard, "I don' know, señor, they've covered their tracks. Mebbe all of them, mebbe not," he shrugged his shoulders, hands out at his side.

Tate slowly drew his bead, took in a breath, let part out and slowly squeezed the trigger. The big Spencer bucked, and the thunderous roar bounced back and forth between the granite walls of the canyon. The big flat-topped saddle horn of the bandido exploded just as he reached for it to mount his horse. The long-maned black spooked and spun around leaving the canyon with mane and tail flying and the Mexican running after him, shouting and waving. The horse that had stood beside the black set to bucking and his rider jammed his boots deep in the tapaderos and fought to pull the horse's head up, but the dapple grey was determined to get rid of his rider and to follow his friend down the canyon. The horse had buried his muzzle between his front legs and stretched his hind legs toward the clouds, and with each buck, made it further from the others, but was unsuccessful in unseating his rider. They soon disappeared down the draw as Tate brought his eyes to the remaining outlaws.

Bull and the other men had taken cover and were searching for the source of the rifle fire. Tate saw the boot of one of the men sticking out past the edge of his covering boulder, and he took aim, quickly squeezed off another shot that shattered the boot heel of the man, but Tate didn't see it, as he was already on his way to another position. Gunfire rattled from below and the twang of ricocheting bullets echoed across the canyon.

But Tate wasn't where they were shooting, and when they rose from behind cover to try to score a hit on the unseen shooter, Tate's Spencer burned a trail across the back of Bull with a .52 caliber slug that tore the back of his shirt off. The big man jumped and yowled like a lonesome prairie wolf and danced like an Apache at his war dance. Tate drew his Colt and added to the excitement by throwing a few random rounds in the vicinity of the dancer. As he did, he saw another of the men with Bull, straddle his mount and high tail it down the canyon. Tate drew back, took another position back to his left and behind a scrub piñon, watching the action of those in the arroyo bottom. Before long, the two remaining riders, one limping on a heel-less boot, mounted up and lying low on their horses' necks, left the canyon at a full gallop as Bull shouted and screamed at their backs.

Bull hollered up from the bottom, "Hey! Whoever's up there shootin', I'm hurt an' need a doctor!"

Tate answered, cupping his hands to his mouth, "You can find one in Santa Fe!"

"But I'm hit! Don't know if I can make it!" he answered.

"Then sit down an' bleed out, your choice!"

"What about my gold?" he asked, still behind his rock.

"Ain't yours! It belongs to the Union Army! You stole a bag!"

After a few moments of silence, "Alright! I'm leavin'! Don't shoot no more!" he whined, peeking out from behind the rock, trying to see his shooter.

"Leave your rifle!" ordered Tate.

Bull started from behind the big rock, looking up at the rim-rock where he suspected the shooter was seated, still holding his rifle. Tate stepped out, rifle in hand, "Leave your rifle!" he ordered again.

Bull looked down at the weapon, back up to Tate, "But, I'll need it!" he wailed, slowly raising the muzzle.

Tate knew what was coming and dropped to one knee as he

brought up the Spencer. Bull's Springfield barked, but he rushed his shot and as the bullet whined overhead, Tate's rifle roared, spitting lead and smoke, and the big slug rocked Bull back against the boulder. He grabbed at his chest, looked up at Tate and slid down the big rock, falling forward on his face, unmoving.

Tate was still, watching, then shook his head and mumbled, "He just wouldn't learn."

THEY RODE ALL NIGHT, taking short breaks to give the horses a breather now and then, and just as he started looking for a place to stop and have some coffee and maybe a short snooze, Tate saw Kaniache and the two Baker brothers that had ridden with him. They came from the timber trailing the loaded pack horse and looking a little weary. Tate and Otis had crossed the Pecos River by the grey light of early morning. Now, having rounded the point of the rim-rock plateau that bordered the south side of the wide valley with the Sangre de Cristos to the north, the thinning timber yielded to the approach of Kaniache and company. They had dropped off the plateau, bound for the roadway that would lead them to Las Vegas.

Tate lifted a hand to wave them over and together they made a camp, stripping and tethering the horses, and starting enough of a fire for some coffee and maybe some pork belly and Johnny cakes. The coffee had just begun to perk when they were hailed by Hoback and company, who gladly joined them for some breakfast.

As Hoback stretched out, head against the log, Tate asked, "Any trouble?"

"Nope. Did hear a spot of shootin' north of us, but too far away and not much of it. Thot it best to keep comin', what with the cargo we gots."

"You did right. Coulda been anything," surmised Tate.

"Ummhumm, thot it mighta been Mac, but was only 'bout half-dozen shots, then nothin'. If we coulda found em, it'd been too late to help. If'n it was him, should see 'im soon, though," added Hoback from under his hat. He folded his hands across his chest and before Tate could ask any more, he began to snore.

Tate chuckled, shaking his head as he grinned and reached for the coffee.

CHAPTER TWENTY-NINE
UNION

THE FIRST SIGHT OF FORT UNION SURPRISED TATE, ALTHOUGH THEY had come near the fort when the freighters traveled to Santa Fe, this was his first time to the most northern fort in New Mexico territory. Arrayed on the west side of the star-shaped earthwork fortress, were two long rows of wall tents that housed the almost one thousand New Mexico volunteers. The Third Cavalry regulars, under Major Duncan, had been ordered east and the post was now manned exclusively by the volunteers under Colonel Benjamin Roberts and Colonel Miguel Pino, the hero of the Valverde battle. Tate's orders were to deliver the gold to Colonel Roberts, and he led his small entourage through the heavy gates of the fort.

He looked around as they entered, seeing gun positions, several cannon, and bunker-like quarters and storehouses. They were directed to the quartermaster's warehouse and as Tate reined up before the large barn-style doors, he was greeted by an officer, "Tate Saint, I presume?"

Tate swung a leg over Shady's rump and stepped toward the man, obviously a high-ranking officer but without his uniform jacket, and extended his hand to shake. "That's right. And who might I be addressing?"

The older man chuckled, shook Tate's hand and answered, "I'm Colonel Benjamin Roberts, commandant of Fort Union. I believe you have a shipment for me?"

"Yessir, and pleased I am to be rid of it! But of course, these men," motioning to the grinning and anxious miners, still mounted and holding tight to the leads of the packhorses, "are anxious to be paid."

"Fine, fine," the Colonel answered, then turning to a man at his side that stood in uniform britches, galluses over his tattered union suit, and thumbs inserted behind them, "This is our quartermaster, McGillicutty. He'll check the weight and such and when I get his report, the money will be dispersed."

Tate turned to Mac, who had caught up with them at Las Vegas, giving a report of a brief skirmish with some Confederate deserters, and said, "Mac, you an' the professor stay with the goods, make sure the count is correct and you can bring the report to the Colonel's office."

The Colonel frowned, "Now, just a minute . . ." he began to question, but Tate held up his hand, "Colonel, that's First Sergeant McIntosh out of Carson's command at Fort Stanton. He's one of your regulars."

"Oh, oh, alright then," sputtered the Colonel. "McGillicutty will show you to my office." He turned to Tate, "Perhaps you and these others might like to have a drink or something to eat. The Sutler has both a bar and serves some pretty decent fare."

Tate nodded his head, motioned to the men to join him, and led the way to the bar. When the men had ordered and all were seated at the long plank table with benches, Tate lifted his cup to a toast, "Here's to a successful mission! Thank you one and all!"

All the men raised their cups or mugs and said together, "Here! Here!" happily agreeing with the toast. Dutch leaned over near Tate, looked in his cup, "That's coffee!" he exclaimed. "What's the matter, you ain't too good to drink with us, are you?" He wasn't trying to be belligerent, just curious, as he looked to the man that had led them for the past week.

Tate dropped his eyes, chuckled, "Not at all. I've tried that stuff," nodding to the mugs and glasses of whiskey and beer, "just don't like it. Can't understand why anyone would choke that stuff down when it tastes worse'n water from a stagnant pond, an' more like lickin' sap off'n a pine tree, when they could have pure mountain spring water or a cup of Arbuckle's. Just a matter of taste's all."

The men laughed, most agreeing with him, as Tate stood at the end of the table, "Men, I'm gonna be pushin' off soon's I replenish my supplies" but before he could finish his good-bye speech, the door pushed open and Mac and the professor came in grinning, followed by a young Lieutenant Hathaway. The anxious Lieutenant interrupted, "I'm in charge of disbursements. Those of you that are the miners and due payment, step over here to the counter." He went to the counter, stepped behind it and lay out a paper and sat a bag that, by the sound of it, had gold coin. The excited miners lined up, listened to the tally, grinned and quickly signed their names and took the payment. They returned to the table and a smiling Professor asked, "Now, where were you, Tate?"

Tate grinned at the man, "Well, I was sayin', I'm anxious to be gettin' back to my woman and family, so, I'll be leavin' directly. But, I want you to know, I've been pleased to be with you all this past week." The others nodded, commenting and reciprocating the words of appreciation. "So, where'bouts you all headed?"

The professor was the first to speak up, "Me'n these two ya-hoos," pointing to the brothers Baker, "We're headin' out to Californy. Ain't made up our minds if'n we're goin' into some kinda business, the gold-fields, or just findin' a good woman and settlin' down!"

Dutch grinned, "I'm goin' to Nebraska Territory! They say there's good farmland and I shall get me a goot farm, a goot woman, and raise crops and children, Jah!"

The others had similar plans, two were returning to the east, and one planned to join a wagon train and go to Oregon. Tate looked to Mac and Hoback, "You?" he asked.

Mac grinned, "The lieutenant there already gave me an' Hoback our orders. We're goin' to Fort Sumner an' help keep them Mescalero busy on Bosque Redondo!"

Tate looked at the group, "You're all good men and if you're ever up in Wind River Mountain country, look me up!"

Each of the men stood, went to Tate and shook his hand and bid their good-byes. Tate went to the Sutler's counter and gave him a list of needed supplies, and as they were assembled, he settled up and within a short time, had the new supplies on the packhorse and was ready to leave. Mac and the professor, following the quartermaster, stopped and said their good-byes, and Tate reined around to leave the fort.

HE KNEW it was about a two-day trip to Taos and the home of Kit Carson. He started out due west until he came to the Mora river, then followed the river north to the mountains. When the river bent back to the west and broke through a long hog-back ridge, Tate found himself in a beautiful and fertile valley. The sun had dropped below the ragged Sangre de Cristo mountains and dusk brought a touch of mountain chill, prompting Tate to stop for some coffee and maybe a fresh tin of peaches. He looked around at the beginning of the black timber, the granite peaks in the distance, and breathed deep of the mountain air, something he had been missing with the time in the desert. It had been a long day and he decided to make a camp for the night and enjoy the mountains in the daytime on the morrow.

It was still dark when he rousted about, rigged the horses, and with a wave to Lobo, took to the trail. He knew he would follow the Mora until he came to a cut on the west side of a valley that held a trail to a mountain pass that crossed these lower mountains of the Sangre de Cristos. By late afternoon, he was across the pass and having followed the edge of the trees north, he dropped into the valley of Taos. Within a short while, he rode up to the ranch house of his friend. A long low adobe with a sweeping veranda, the dirty blonde hair of Carson caught the slight breeze as he lifted a hand to wave his friend near.

"Bout time you got here! I was beginnin' to wonder!" he said as he greeted Tate. He stepped off the porch and walked to the hitch rail, took the lead of the pack horse as Tate stepped down, and said, "We'll put 'em in the barn," and led off around the house.

BOTH MEN CRADLED the hot cups of steaming traditional Mexican coffee tasting of cinnamon and sugar. Tate took his first sip, smiled and looked at Josefa as she sat beside Kit, "This is delicious! I've never had it before, what do you call it?"

"It is Café de Olla. We make it in a clay pot, and it is one of my husband's favorites," she answered, speaking so softly Tate struggled to hear.

"I like it!" declared Tate, taking another sip.

"Just one of the many reasons I'm glad to be home!" stated Kit, reaching over to touch his wife's hand.

"So, you really did it? Resigned, I mean," asked Tate. "How did the general respond?"

"Oh, he wasn't happy. Not at all, tried to get me to change my mind. But after his order about the Mescalero, I had my stomach full!" spat Carson. "But, I'm thinkin' it was good we were there. If he'd sent some o' them eager West Pointers, they'd probably followed his orders to the letter and there'd be dead Mescalero scattered all over this country!"

Tate sipped his coffee, looked to Kit, "There kinda is anyway!"

Carson sputtered, and exclaimed, "But not as many as there would'a been!"

"You're prob'ly right about that. Do you think they'll do alright at Bosque Redondo?"

"You know Tate, that's one o' the problems with these generals an' others that don't know what it is to hunt for their supper. Now, don't get me wrong, the Bosque is fine country, but with that many Apache livin' there, all the game'll be hunted off all too soon. And the general's thinkin' there's room for more! He promised the leaders that the government'll keep 'em fat an' happy, but he just don't understand! This is his great experiment and he thinks he'll get a feather in his cap just 'cuz of it. But he don't care 'bout them people! And I get the impression he'll wanna put every Indian in New Mexico territory on that one reservation! Either that or he'll try to kill 'em all off, like he wanted us to do!" grumbled the Colonel.

Tate thought about things a moment, then asked, "You mean, he's gonna want to put the Navajo on there with 'em?"

Kit nodded his head slowly, "And there's about ten times more Navajo than Mescalero. And then there's the other bands of the Apache, the Chiricahua, Mimbres, Lipan, and more. But the biggest bunch is the Navajo!"

"Ain't the Navajo an' the Apache enemies?" asked Tate.

Kit sipped his coffee as he nodded his head, "Ummmhumm, they are."

"So," considered Tate, thinking about the many settlements of the Navajo, "he really would try to wipe 'em out."

"Ummhumm, that's his way," answered Kit.

ONCE TATE FINISHED his coffee and the conversation waned, he stood, stretched, and looking to his friend, "I think I'm gonna hit the trail. Good moon tonight and the wind's settled down, so travel will be good."

Josefa looked at Tate, "But it's getting dark!" she declared, not understanding.

Kit chuckled, put his hand on his wife's knee, "Tate likes to travel at night. I think he's second cousin to them owls out there." He grinned and stood, "Let me walk with you to the stable." Tate nodded, then speaking to Josefa, "Ma'am, thank you for that mighty fine meal. An' you take care o' this man, he's a keeper!"

She smiled and nodded, excused herself and picked up the cups to return into the house. Tate and Kit walked silently to the barn and Carson watched as his friend geared up the pack horse and saddled Shady. Lobo had lounged in the barn with Shady and now sat, tongue lolling, waiting on Tate. "Did you hear about Mangas Coloradas?" asked Kit, watching his friend.

"No, can't say as I did. What about him?"

"He decided to turn himself in, down to Fort McLane and sue for peace. He was made promises and he returned with his people under a flag of truce to meet with General Joe West, one o' them California militia men. But West said he wanted him dead, so that night his men took ol' Mangas out, said he was 'escaping' and tortured and killed him. Then they cut off his head, boiled it, and they done sent it to some scientist name o' Fowler in New York City."

Tate paused, looking down, shook his head. "No wonder none of 'em wanna trust the white man."

"Ain't that the truth!" responded Carson.

Kit looked to Tate, "Thanks for coming my friend, you've been a great help."

Tate turned, shook the Colonel's hand, "Anytime, Kit. You've been a great friend and you know I can't say no to you." Tate climbed aboard, looked down at his friend one last time, and with a wave to Lobo, he rode from the home of Kit and Josefa, turning once in his saddle for a last wave to his friend.

CHAPTER THIRTY
HOME

THE LAST HINT OF LIGHT USHERED TATE FROM TAOS. AS HE RODE BY the ancient Taos Pueblo, the shadows stretched across the four storied adobe structure, where sat several of the residents on the differing rooftop verandas, enjoying the cool of the evening. Tate reined Shady to the shoulder of the mountain that pointed west to the Rio Grande canyon, and let Lobo range far ahead as he thought the mountains of the Sangre de Cristos were already smiling their approval of the lone traveler. He was nearing familiar country and planned to stop at their southern cabin just north of the massive sand dunes on the east edge of the historic San Luis valley.

He guessed it would be approaching sunrise when he rode past Fort Garland and would see the beginning of a new day within recognizable country. As anxious as he felt, he knew he would have to take his time and not wear out Shady and the pack horse. It would take just over two weeks to make it home, but traveling through mountain country and familiar lands, sure beat that desert.

But it was mid-morning after another long night's journey that Tate rode the tree line overlooking the sand dunes. With every step, he remembered the times spent here, from his very first year in the mountains, and the many times afterward. As he rode into the clearing that held his cabin, he was surprised to see horses in the corral and smoke coming from the chimney. He reined up back in the trees, and looked all around, seeing no one, but assuming they, whoever they were, were in the cabin. He lifted his eyes to the sky, guessing it to be about an hour before sunrise, and assumed they were preparing their morning meal. He stood in his stirrups, looking at the horses, three, in the corral. They looked like good stock, well taken care of, and fat. A hide was stretched and pegged on the ground, scraped clean. Tate called out, "Hello, the house! Anybody home?"

The door was pulled open just a crack and a rifle barrel protruded before a voice answered, "Who's there?" It was a woman's voice and sounded young as well.

"The name's Saint! Tate Saint! And who might you be?" he asked.

"Just never you mind!" she declared. "Now git! We don't want'chu here!"

Tate gave a little leg pressure to Shady, moving into the clearing, "You livin' here, are you?" he called, watching the door closely and looking around for any others. He sat easy in the saddle, one hand on the horn and the other resting on his thigh.

"Why're you here?" called the woman.

"Well, ma'am, I was plannin' on spendin' the day in my cabin, and catchin' up on my sleep."

"Your cabin?" squeaked the surprised woman.

"That's right. I built that cabin. Lived in it quite a few years. And if you'll look at the corner of that split log table, you'll see the initials T.S. carved."

The woman was silent for a moment but didn't move. "That could be anybody! Tom Smith or such."

Tate grinned, dropped his head, then with another thought, "And over the mantle of the fireplace, right in the center, is a big piece of shiny black Onyx."

Again, the woman paused, "Are you alone?"

"Yes ma'am. But, tell you what, how 'bout I just bed down in the shed yonder. Long's I got some shelter from this wind, I'll be fine." He waited a moment for her response, then started to rein Shady toward the shed, but the woman pushed open the door, still holding the rifle ready and stepped on the porch.

"I've got some biscuits and some pork-belly on, if'n you'd like," she offered.

Tate grinned, "Now that's an invitation I'd not turn down. I'll just put my horses in the corral, and be right there, ma'am, if'n that's alright?"

She nodded, and turned away, stepping back through the door. When Tate finished stripping the packs and saddle from the horses, he rubbed them down and turned them into the second corral. He swung the saddle and packs to the top rail, and with rifle and bow in hand, he walked to the porch. After a knock and a bid to come in, he walked into the familiar room of his first cabin.

Seated at the table were a man with a splint on a leg and another on his arm, two youngsters, a boy and girl were on the side of the table with the long bench. The man waved to the seat at the end and Tate, after hanging his hat on the peg and leaning the rifle and bow against the wall near the door, started to the table. Extending his hand, he said, "I'm Tate Saint."

The man grinned and stretched out to grasp Tate's hand saying, "I'm Michael Fitzgerald, this is my wife, Madeline, and this is my son, Matthew and daughter, Melissa or Missy." Tate nodded to each one before sitting and watched as Madeline or Maddy, served everyone, beginning with her husband. When she was seated, the family joined hands and Michael led in prayer, thanking the Lord for a new day and the blessings they enjoyed. As he said "Amen," he was echoed by the family and Tate and the boy asked, "Did you build this cabin?"

Tate chuckled, "Yes, I did. And I wasn't much older'n you when I did!"

"Wow! That musta been a long time ago!" declared the wide-eyed boy.

"Were you planning on taking possession of the cabin, Mr. Saint?" asked Michael.

Tate shook his head as he placed a piece of pork belly on a biscuit, "No, not now. I'm just passing through, headin' to my home in the Wind River Mountains, further north."

The relief showed on both Michael and Maddy's faces at his explanation, but Michael continued, "We weren't planning on staying, but with the accident, it was difficult to travel. The wagonmaster said he thought there was a cabin up here and we might try to stay 'till I healed up, so . . ." he shrugged his shoulders as he explained.

"What happened?" asked Tate, slowing not at all with his eating.

"Hit a hole with the wagon, knocked me plumb off the seat and went tumblin' down the side hill through the rocks. Broke the wheel and cracked the axle. Got a spare wheel, but the axle's a different story. By trade, I'm a blacksmith, but with this," nodding toward his arm and leg, "can't do much till I get better. The folks on the train helped get the wagon into the trees down below, but . . ."

"Where were you headed, Oregon?" asked Tate.

"We were, but with this, it'll be too late to try. So, I dunno," he added, looking to his wife as she reached out to take his hand. "Whatever the Lord has in mind, I guess."

"Were you going to be a smitty in Oregon or were you plannin' on farmin'?" asked Tate.

"Whatever it would take to make a living."

Tate wiped his plate clean with the last biscuit, picked up his coffee cup, looked to Maddy, "Fine breakfast ma'am. Mighty fine. Thank you!" He looked to Michael, "Ever tried prospectin'? You know, for gold?"

"Thought of it, just like everything else, but I just don't know."

Tate leaned back in his seat, "Tell ya' what. You all seem like fine folks, and you can stay here long's you need. There's plenty of game in the mountains, but there's Ute, Comanche, and Apache Indians all around. Now the closest settlement of any kind is San Luis to the south, Hardscrabble back over these mountains, that trail down in the draw yonder," he nodded toward the break in the mountains that held the small stream, "that's called Music Pass, but there's 'nother'n south a mite called Medano Pass. Then, of course, there's Bent's Fort but if'n you go north through this valley, the trail drops down another pass an' comes out at a little settlement they're callin' Poncha Springs. But, an' here's the deal, back up the valley yonder, there's a couple streams you might pan a little gold."

They continued talking about the valley and the possibility of gold. Tate enjoyed telling them about the area, the hot springs, the water falls to the south, and the many places where they could find game.

Maddy looked to Tate, "But, if there's gold there, why tell us? Why don't you get it?"

Tate grinned, "Well, it just never interested me. I don't need it, don't want to take the time to get it, and I already have everything I need. 'Sides, I'm anxious to get home to my family. But if you folks wanna give it a try, have at it. But, you'll prob'ly wanna build yourself a cabin nearby up there. I don't know when we'll be coming back here, but I'm sure we will. My Maggie sets store by this place, bein' our first home an' all."

After he explained about traveling at night and how he needed to get some sleep, they let him go to the shed and throw out his bedroll. He was glad for the time to rest, unconcerned about attacking Apache, and was soon deep in sleep.

He was awakened by Lobo as the boy Matthew approached the open-ended shed, and he sat up, watching the boy near. When Matthew saw Tate was awake, "Ma says for you to come to dinner. It's almost ready!" he declared.

Tate chuckled, "Tell your Ma, thanks. I'll be right in."

AFTER A PLEASANT MEAL of turkey taken by Matthew, Tate geared up and readied to take to the trail. The family stood close as he mounted up and after their good-byes, Tate took to the familiar trail that would lead from the valley and into the northern mountains. With a wave over his shoulder, he heard them shout another "Goodbye and God speed," and with a smile, he soon broke from the trees, facing the disappearing sun that threw lances of gold across the sky to bid farewell to another day.

It was two weeks of enjoyable travel that brought Tate through the mountains of the new named Colorado territory and into what had been the unorganized territory but was now changing almost every year. But Tate did not concern himself with any other names besides home. He came within sight of the few cabins called South Pass Station, and needing no supplies chose not to stop, and with the sun barely threatening to rise, he pushed on into the black timber that rose on the flanks of the mountains before him.

As the sun boldly showed itself and bent the first rays over the eastern edge of the mountains, Tate reined up in the black timber at the crest of the hill. He leaned forward on the pommel of the saddle and took in the view before him, one he never tired of absorbing. The deep blue beneath the mirror smooth of the waters of the lake lay undisturbed, reflecting the hills beyond. A thin wisp of smoke rose from the chimney and Tate pictured Maggie busy at the hearth fixing her biscuits in the dutch oven. The black form of the wolf, Indy, lay on the porch, head between his paws, staring toward the lake. The corral was empty, and he knew the horses would be in the back pasture. He sidestepped Shady away from the big ponderosa and was a little surprised to see a second cabin, not quite completed, behind and beyond the familiar place. He recognized another figure, Sean, coming from behind the cabin, carrying an armload of firewood. With a heavy sigh that lifted his shoulders, he gigged Shady forward, and looking to Lobo, "Let's go home, boys!"

He reined wide around the place and dropped from the trees into the upper pasture. They quietly approached the open-ended barn from behind the cabin, and stepped down, just as Indy came running around the corner to greet Lobo. The two wolves sniffed, ran in circles, and rolled on the ground as they greeted one another. Tate chuckled as he stripped the horses, hanging the gear in the barn and the packs from the top rail of the adjoining fence. With rifle, bow, quiver and saddlebags in hand, he padded around the house and quietly stepped up on the porch. He sat down his arm-load beside the door and hearing the chatter of those inside, he quietly pushed the door open and stepped inside. All three women were busy at the counter, talking and preparing for the meal, backs to the door, but Sean saw his dad and started to jump up but was stopped when Tate held a finger to his lips.

Sean relaxed, grinning, and watched Tate move behind Maggie, slip his arms around her waist and say, "What's for breakfast, woman!"

Maggie jumped, and turned around, and instantly wrapped her arms around him and hugged him as tight as she could. The other women, both startled, stepped back and seeing Maggie's response, knew who was there and they smiled, holding hands to their mouths as they watched the reunion. Maggie leaned back, both hands holding his face as she stared into his eyes, "Oh, it is so good to see you!" then wrapped her arms around his neck again and pulled his face down for another lingering kiss.

Although the table was loaded with food, there was more talking than eating as they struggled to share everything in such a short time. As Sean told of White Fox and how she had been stolen as a child, Tate's brow wrinkled as he listened. He looked to White Fox, "Do you remember the names of your parents in Santa Fe?"

"Yes, I do. He was a trader and she was from Santa Fe. His name was Felix Fraser and her name was Juanita. But they were killed when I was taken by the Comanche."

Tate thought a moment, then said, "No, they weren't. I met them in Santa Fe."

White Fox's eyes grew wide, and she looked to Sean and back to Tate, "You met them? How?"

Tate told of the two youngsters from the wagon train and how he asked the Padre to help find them a home. He told how they were taken in by a couple who lost their daughter many years ago in a Comanche raid, and they still grieved for her. "We will have to get word to them, if you want."

She looked afraid, but curious, and looked to Sean, who nodded his head in approval, "Yes, yes, I would like that."

There were many other things talked about, but Tate finally had to say, "Look, I've traveled all night and I'm in need of some sleep, but first, I want to just sit on the porch and relax. How 'bout we take our coffee out there?"

All agreed, and within a few moments, Tate, Maggie, Sean, White Fox, and Sadie were joined by Lobo and Indy, as they sat quietly together, enjoying the cool morning of the Wind River Mountains. It was good to be home.

LOOK FOR DI NE' DEFIANCE (ROCKY MOUNTAIN SAINT 14)

Coming Soon from B.N. Rundell and Wolfpack Publishing

ABOUT THE AUTHOR

Born and raised in Colorado into a family of ranchers and cowboys, B.N. Rundell is the youngest of seven sons. Juggling bull riding, skiing, and high school, graduation was a launching pad for a hitch in the Army Paratroopers. After the army, he finished his college education in Springfield, MO, and together with his wife and growing family, entered the ministry as a Baptist preacher.

Together, B.N. and Dawn raised four girls that are now married and have made them proud grandparents. With many years as a successful pastor and educator, he retired from the ministry and followed in the footsteps of his entrepreneurial father and started a successful insurance agency, which is now in the hands of his trusted nephew. He has also been a successful audiobook narrator and has recorded many books for several award-winning authors. Now finally realizing his life-long dream, B.N. has turned his efforts to writing a variety of books, from children's picture books and young adult adventure books, to the historical fiction and western genres.